SHOSHONE SUMMER

STONECROFT SAGA 8

B.N. RUNDELL

WOLFPACK
PUBLISHING
— EST 2010 —

WOLFPACK
PUBLISHING
— EST 2013 —

Shoshone Summer

Paperback Edition
Copyright © 2020 B.N. Rundell

Wolfpack Publishing
6032 Wheat Penny Avenue
Las Vegas, NV 89122

wolfpackpublishing.com

Paperback ISBN 978-1-64734-055-1
eBook ISBN 978-1-64734-054-4

Library of Congress Control Number: 2020942438

SHOSHONE SUMMER

1 / SETTLING

The big black wolf stretched his head to the dusky sky and howled, huffed, and let his howl rise higher and be carried by the evening breeze. The big moon was rising in the east, a few stars had lit their lanterns, and the wolf howled again. Far away, an answering cry lifted and the black wolf, orange eyes blazing in the dim light, turned to look at his friend, the broad shouldered dark-blonde-haired buckskin attired man, the man that had raised him from a pup found in the cavern behind his cabin, the man known as Gabe Stone.

Gabe had watched Wolf lift his night song to the stars, smiled, and when the wolf looked back at him, he lifted his head in assent. The wolf looked to the distant call, gave another turn to look at his friend, then trotted off the stony knoll and into the woods beyond. Gabe chuckled, shook his head, and whispered to the night, "Don't forget where home is boy."

He came to the crest of the knoll to watch the Creator paint the western sky with the broad brush of color. Orange, gold, yellow and red were splashed across the wide sky that was impaled on the granite tipped peaks of the Wind River mountains, the mountains that had become the home of Gabe and his friend, Ezra and his wife, Grey Dove. Gabe and Ezra had been friends since they ran the woods of Pennsylvania together as boys barely out of their knee britches. They had traveled together when Gabe was forced to leave Philadelphia after an unfortunate outcome of a duel, fought over the honor of Gabe's sister. The duel resulted in the father of the dead man placing an unlawful bounty on Gabe's head and he chose to leave to protect his family. But the two men had longed for and dreamed of exploring the wilderness of the west most of their lives and they took advantage of the situation to fulfill that long held dream.

Gabe smiled at the many memories and watched the colors of the sunset fade, leaving only the silhouette of the mountain range against the fading blue and grey of the night sky. He lifted his head and watched as more stars lit their lanterns, watched the slow rise of the moon, and remembered the many times he and his wife, Pale Otter had sat together enjoying the night sky. But Otter was gone, killed by a renegade Bannock that thought no woman of the Shoshone should be the woman of a white man. But Gabe had his revenge in a fight with the man, a fight that resulted in the death of the man, but not at Gabe's hand. Now he was alone, living in the cabin he and Ezra had built for their new wives, sisters of the Shoshone people. Maybe he should take another woman to wife, but the thought of another woman taking the place of his Pale Otter just didn't sit well with him, and he rose from his cold seat on the lichen covered boulder, lifted his eyes again to the night sky and started back to the cabin, certain that Grey Dove, Ezra and their new son, waited for him.

As he stepped through the door, the fire in the fireplace illumined the interior, showing the table and chairs, two larger chairs with cushions, the counter that held the pans, pots and utensils, and Ezra and Dove, both busy at the table and fire. The furnishings were the first effort by the men at making any furniture items, and though somewhat rough in design, it was sturdy and served the purpose.

Dove smiled as Gabe entered, looked behind him and asked, "Where is Wolf? Is he not with you?"

Gabe chuckled, "Nah, he was talking to a she wolf up in the hills and he decided to go courtin'!"

Dove frowned, "Courting?"

Ezra chimed in, "You know, lookin' for a female friend."

Dove smiled, nodded, and turned to her work at the fire with the pot of stew and more.

As they sat at supper, Ezra looked at his friend, "So, you thought any more about it?"

Gabe frowned, took another bite of elk meat from the stew, looked at Ezra with a questioning look, "It?"

"The gathering. Dove wants us to go with her people to the grand encampment of the Shoshone. It's gonna be up north near where we were when you left."

"You sure you wanna make that trip with little Chipmunk there?" nodding to the babe in the papoose carrier.

Both Ezra and Dove looked at Gabe with a slight frown until Dove asked, "Is that your chosen name?"

Gabe grinned. "Well, I did consider Skunk or somethin' more descriptive, but . . ." he glanced at Ezra who shook his head, knowing the mischievousness of his friend. Then with eyes slit and a firm set of his jaw, "If you tried to hang a name like that on my son, we'd have to have us a talk outside!"

Both Gabe and Dove laughed, as she handed the cradle board to Gabe for a closer look at the little one, but when the child wrinkled up and showed dark eyes that were ready to burst the tear dam, he handed the board back, relieved. Since his return after his journey back to St. Louis to settle some family matters, he had been tasked as the official uncle of the newborn with the responsibility of naming the child. The names given to the little ones were carried until they earned their permanent name, usually in their teen years and after some vision quest or special happening that manifested the new name. Gabe had thought about it for several days, and each time he looked at the youngster, he was reminded of the playful antics of the mountain chipmunk that was always stealing tidbits of food, or chattering at those around and expressing his disapproval at their interference in his life and home. He thought the name fit the little tyke who had done much the same in making himself heard.

Gabe looked at Dove, "Don't you think it fits?"

Dove looked from Gabe to the boy in the carrier, who was smiling and playing with a rattle made by his father out of a dried gourd, then to her husband, Ezra. "Yes. I have thought the same. When he is hungry, he sounds much like an upset chipmunk!"

Ezra laughed, "Let's just hope he doesn't get in the habit of stealing whatever he wants when he wants it." Ezra looked to his friend, "So, you wanna go, or not?"

"You mean to the encampment? Sure, I haven't set a horse for a long ride in, oh, two or three days. My posterior oughta be healed up by now!"

"Ha! Leather britches! You don't have a posterior, you've got calluses!" retorted Ezra, throwing a scrap of buckskin at his friend.

***

The men sat on the bench outside, enjoying the cool night air as they sipped the last of the coffee. Ezra turned to Gabe and asked, "You ever gonna tell me 'bout your trip to St. Louis, or you just gonna keep me in the dark?"

Gabe grinned, sipped his coffee and remembered, reached into this tunic and pulled out a letter, "This came for you from your Pa."

Ezra frowned, "What'd he say?"

Gabe shook his head, "How do I know, I didn't read it!" Gabe lifted the steaming cup to his lips as Ezra sat his down and tore open the letter and started reading by the dim light of the full moon.

As he finished, he grinned, folded it up and put it in his pocket, looked to Gabe, "Ever'things fine! Church is still growin', they're happy together, as always, and he said to come home if'n I was of a mind to, but if not, to be happy where I am!" His father was the pastor of the largest church for coloreds in the east, the Mother Bethel African Methodist Episcopal Church of Philadelphia.

"You need to write 'em next chance you get, tell about Chipmunk," suggested Gabe.

"Yeah, s'pose so. Now, what about the trip?"

"Ah, tweren't nothin' much. Met a woman, she wanted to get married, I didn't. Had a couple run-ins with bounty hunters, left 'em lay. Came upriver on a keelboat of Choteau's, came across land to home."

"That's it? Gone nigh unto a year, an' that's it?" questioned a flabbergasted Ezra, shaking his head.

"Pretty much," answered Gabe. "Kinda boring." He drank the last of the coffee, tossed out the dregs and sat back to look at the stars. After a moment he turned to Ezra, "So, if we go to this grand encampment, do we have to travel with the village yonder, or can we kinda scout out our own way?"

Ezra thought a moment, "Reckon we can go our own way, but why you bein' so unsociable?"

Gabe chuckled, "Coz every married woman in that village will be tryin' to get me hitched 'fore summer's over! And more'n likely, to the homeliest woman in the entire tribe!"

2 / PREPARATIONS

When Gabe stepped through the door of the cabin, he almost tripped over the lazing Wolf who snoozed just outside the door. The dim light of pre-dawn showed the black form and Gabe did a quick hop over the sleeping form, only to have Wolf rise behind him to follow on his morning jaunt. It had always before been Gabe's routine to circle behind the big stone monolith that sheltered their cavern/cabin and welcome the morning as he sat on the crest of the rocky shoulder. The sunrise in the mountains was his favorite time and he preferred to spend those moments with his Lord in prayer. Now with Wolf at his side, he mounted the shoulder and took his seat on the cold lichen covered stone, laying his Bible beside him as he looked to the changing colors in the eastern sky.

He looked down the valley of the Popo Agie, broad shoulders of the foothills framing the view, the south end of the Wind River valley the shadowy base of the picturesque unfolding panorama. The cool morning air nipped at his neck, moving the long somewhat curly hair around to slap his face, as it tumbled from the mountains behind him. As he started his prayer, he was nudged by the big wolf, insistent for attention, and a whimper that told of some concern. He tried to focus on his thoughts, but Wolf nudged again, started moving away and stopped to look back, then started on again. Wolf was not one to just want attention, and this kind of behavior told him something was wrong. He rose to follow, and Wolf quickened his pace and he trotted back to the front of the cabin.

Ezra had just stepped outside and stood stretching when Wolf and Gabe came near. He frowned, bent to stroke the scruff of the wolf and looked to Gabe, who was scowling as he followed the black wolf. "What's wrong?" queried Ezra, knowing the expression on his friend's face told of some concern.

"Dunno, Wolf's naggin' at me and bid me follow, so ..."

Wolf looked from one man to the other, trotted away, stopped and looked back, raising his head with a slight whine, and stared at the two with a look that was more than a bid, closer to a demand for them to follow.

Gabe looked to Ezra, "You get our rifles and gear, I'll follow." He patted the butt of his belt pistol, the Bailes over/under double barreled flinter, "I've got this, but don't waste time coming."

Ezra nodded, watched for a moment to see where Wolf led them, then ducked into the cabin to retrieve the rifles and possibles pouches. He grabbed his Lancaster .54 caliber rifle, swung the strap with his possibles bag over his shoulder, stepped to the door of the second room, picked up Gabe's Ferguson rifle and his possibles bag, and started to the door, all the while telling Dove what was going on and that they were in pursuit of Wolf.

"Your meal will be waiting!" she declared as he went through the door.

Gabe broke into a dogtrot, headed up the trail taken by Wolf and Gabe, the trail that led to the upper pasture where they had taken the horses just yesterday. His first thought was there was something after the horses, although he was certain they would stay in the grassy basin. They had reinforced the natural barriers of brush and trees, just to keep the animals from wandering, but not enough to prevent them escaping any danger. He shook his head as he thought of what the cause of Wolf's alarm might be, the wolf was not given to undue concern about anything but was always aware whenever there was legitimate cause for warning.

He caught a glimpse of Gabe and Wolf as they crested the saddle on the trail, quickened his pace and followed. The trail dipped into the thicker black timber but continued on its uphill slant, the trail they followed was a shorter route than the one taken when they rode the horses up to the pasture, but it was also a little more rugged.

As Gabe neared the pasture, he heard the clatter of hooves and the crashing of horses breaking through the brush, he looked to the far edge and heard the bray of the mule, the scream of a horse and the snarl and snapping of wolves. He broke into a run, charging toward the melee and ruckus, grabbing at his pistol as he ran. Wolf loped ahead, but the far edge of the pasture, rimmed by a thick growth of aspen, was about three hundred yards away. Gabe was already winded, but forced himself on, the pistol now in his hand. He brought it to full cock, and he stretched out his long legs trying to catch up to Wolf.

The sound of battle racketed across the grassy basin, squeals, screams, growls, and brays competed in the fracas, and as Gabe neared, he saw the grey form of a wolf fly through the air, and he caught sight of the mule, and knew he had launched the wolf with his hind hooves. But now he had his teeth buried in the neck of another, as two wolves tried repeatedly to ham string him with their fangs, only to meet the sharp hooves as the big mule kicked repeatedly.

Wolf had come to the edge of the pack, lowered his head, bared his fangs and picking his steps, slowly approached the brawl, a growl rumbling from his chest. Two other wolves, both grey but with a splash of black on their backs, turned to face the new challenge. They too dropped to their attack stance, heads lowered, and watching with glaring eyes. The larger of the two, sprung forward, trying their usual tactic where one would distract with a lunging attack, and the other would go for the throat. But Wolf was wary and when the first leaped, he dodged to the right and caught the attack of the second wolf by locking his teeth on the attackers throat, and with one jerk, pulled the throat from his neck, but still had enough of a grip to sling the carcass over his shoulder, just in time to meet the second challenger, head on. The two wolves snarled, growled, and bit, both trying to get a grip on the other's throat or neck, but Wolf was the bigger and stronger of the two and with his second feinting charge, caught the challenger in a death grip just behind his ear, burying his teeth in the grey's neck and with one swift jerk, snapped the bone in the beast's neck, then dropped his carcass at his feet and searched for another.

While Wolf fought his battle and the mule defended himself, Gabe saw another wolf trying for the hind hocks of the mule, and he lifted the pistol, took a quick aim and dropped the hammer. The pistol bucked and roared, spat smoke and lead, and the targeted wolf flinched, whimpered, and trotted off, three legged. Gabe quickly twisted the barrels to bring the unfired one to the top, then cocked the second hammer and looked for another target.

But the remaining wolves had seen Wolf's defeat of their pack leaders and the three backed away from the bloody carcass of the little sorrel, blood dripping from their jowls, as they watched Wolf lift one foot, then another, as he stalked the three remaining predators. Then one, cowered down, chin on the ground as he submitted to Wolf, then the other two did the same. As he walked around them, they showed their submission, tails tucked, heads down, even whimpering. Wolf looked at them as he stood, head high, lips snarling, as he looked around. Then with one quick move, the other three slipped away into the woods. Wolf watched, then turned to look at Gabe and trot to his side.

Gabe looked around, saw two twisted forms of grey fur lying away from the scene of the battle, walked to them and knew they had been done in by the powerful hooves of the mule. One appeared to have been stomped repeatedly, the other was the flying form first seen by Gabe. Two more bloody carcasses lay where Wolf had let them drop, and another dead beast lay in a heap behind the carcass of the horse. Gabe guessed that one had been mauled by the sharp teeth of the mule, but he could not tell for sure. He looked around, five dead wolves, one wounded and would probably die, but three ran off. The best those three could do was find another pack to join, but that could take some time and some travel.

He looked up to see Ezra trotting toward him, a rifle in each hand, and a grin broad enough to compete with the rising sun. "Look's like I got here just in time!" he declared, between breaths. He stopped, handed the Ferguson to Gabe, bent forward with his free hand on a knee and sucked air. In a moment, he stood, looked around, and said, "Not bad, considering you only had that little pea shooter!"

Gabe chuckled, "Tweren't me! The mule done in three, Wolf took care of two, and all I did was wing one and chase it off. Wolf sent the other three away with their tails tucked between their legs."

"You don't say! So, I coulda just walked all the way an' not wear myself out runnin'?"

"Ummhmmm, but I feel a lot better with this in my hands," answered Gabe, hefting his Ferguson rifle. That rifle was his pride and joy, a gift from his father when he left home and a rarity among rifles. It was a breechloader, .62 caliber, and in Gabe's skilled hands, he could get off as many as seven rounds in a minute, compared to the usual three or four of a muzzle loaded rifle such as Ezra's Lancaster.

"Shame about that little sorrel. She was a good horse," declared Ezra. "She was bred by Ebony, but the foal didn't survive, she was a purty one too!"

Gabe looked at the big mule, standing off from them but still skittish and prancing about, he nodded toward the animal, "That one sure did a job, though.

While all the other horses took off, even Ebony, he stayed and fought."

Ezra chuckled, "I'd heard that about mules before. Looks like you got yourself a good one. Can you ride him?"

"Ummhmm, but if you ever rode a mule you know that back bone is far from comfortable. Too skinny behind the withers, unless you got a good saddle or at least a blanket."

"Well, you might hafta ride him to catch up the others. From the looks of things, they tore outta here in a mighty big hurry."

"Can't say's I blame 'em any," answered Gabe, turning to start back to the cabin. He walked to the mule, held out his hand and stroked the mule's head, then his neck, and spoke softly, "C'mon boy, let's go to the cabin." He turned away and started back to the trail that was taken by the horses, for they would need to be gathered up and staked out near the cabin, because today they would start packing things for their journey to the grand encampment.

3 / DEPARTURE

The big black Andalusian stallion stepped out, glad to be under saddle with his long-time friend aboard and trailing the blue roan that had been Pale Otter's ride. The roan gelding was under packsaddles and panniers, not a totally new experience for him having been used as a packhorse by Ezra and Dove on their return from the north country. Behind the roan was Grey Dove aboard her buckskin and trailing the steeldust mustang that dragged the travois loaded with the hide tipi. Ezra brought up the rear aboard his big bay gelding and trailing the wolf-fighting mule who was also under packsaddles and panniers. Wolf took the point, scouting ahead under the direction of Gabe, who grinned at the wolf's enthusiasm to be on the trail again.

It was early afternoon and Gabe expected to travel into the night, anticipating a full moon to light the way for them to make time on this first day out. They were bound for the Wind River valley and would follow the river upstream and climb out of the valley beyond the headwaters of this river and go into the valley of many smokes. They would also be the advance scout for the village of the Shoshone under the leadership of Broken Lance, who would follow the next day. This was all familiar country for Gabe and company, having traveled this way a year ago, but Pale Otter was with them on that journey.

Gabe forcefully tore his thoughts away from the past and the memories of Otter to focus on their journey. Although this was known as Shoshone country, it was not unusual for Crow, Arapaho, Ute, and Blackfoot to make raids into this valley, a valley known for its abundance of game and to also be a summer habitat for buffalo. Because of the many villagers that would be trailing lodge-laden travois, they would keep to the trail that paralleled the Wind River in the bottom of the valley and the travel should be easy. He chuckled at his thoughts of 'easy travel' knowing that nothing is certain and any moment anything could become life threatening. He lifted his eyes to the sky with scattered clouds and felt a light but cool breeze on his face. The breeze came from the mouth of the Popo Agie Canyon where they were bound, but he looked around and saw the quakies shaking their leaves in protest and the juniper swaying as if they expected more to come. Another glance to the clouds, and he detected a darkening to the northwest.

Gabe twisted around in his saddle and called back to Ezra, "Better keep an eye open for shelter in case that wind blows us up a storm!"

Ezra waved a hand in acknowledgment and lifted his eyes to the sky for his own evaluation. His glance at Dove showed she too was looking and judging. But any storm this time of year would only bring rain, even though a heavy cloudburst could do some damage. She was thinking of her planted squash, beans, and corn that she left under the care of her young friend, Little Basket, who would stay behind with the older people that would not make the journey to the grand encampment. There were several others that would also stay, young people that would take care of the remaining horse herd and other planted crops, as well as hunt for meat for the elders. The plan was to return to the valley for the fall hunt and prepare for the cold season, or the months of *yeba mea* and following after the quakies turn gold.

Gabe was remembering what Broken Lance told him about the journey, "This year we go to the land of the *Agaideka,* the Salmon Eaters. And there will be bands from the *Tukkutikka,* the Mountain Sheep Eaters. We of the *Kuccuntikka,* the Buffalo Eaters, had the last gathering in the land of the Wind River. Where we go will be on the Yellowstone River, north of the land of many smokes."

"Will there be others there?" asked Gabe, wondering about the 'great encampment' that others had spoken of, how many bands come from far lands to renew friendships and to visit family members that had married with the other bands.

"There will be some *Boho'inee,* some have taken mates among the Bannock people. And perhaps some *Doyahinee',* they are the Mountain People from the north west. When we had the gathering there were some *Kammitikka,* Jack Rabbit Eaters from the Snake River country. There are bands of the *Newe,* the People, in many places. We are many people."

"So, how long will it take us to get to the gathering place?" asked Gabe.

"This many days," stated Broken Lance, holding up both hands with all fingers, "maybe this many more," holding one hand with all fingers.

Gabe quickly calculated *Fifteen days to get there, a week there, fifteen days back, that'll put us back home before the end of summer.* He nodded his head, "We're leaving now," he motioned to the waiting horses, "so we'll scout things out for you, maybe leave some meat hanging for the people. Any changes, we'll mark the trail with cairns."

"It is good," stated Broken Lance. He had been the leader of the village for just over two years, but this would be their first journey as a village to a grand encampment. His war leader, Chochoco, stood beside him and the men watched Gabe return to the horses and others that waited. When he mounted up, he lifted a hand in farewell, and they started down the trail that followed the Popo Agie River.

As they broke into the open at the mouth of the canyon, Gabe lifted his eyes to the clouds again, reined up and waited for Ezra to come alongside. He pointed to the northwest, "Those clouds look like rainstorm carriers. But they're a long way up the valley, so I figger if we get outta these foothills and into the flats, we could make better time, but, cover's kinda scarce."

"Ah, it's just a rainstorm. You afraid of gettin' wet?" jibed Ezra, grinning at his friend. "That big city livin' make you go soft or sumpin'?"

"You know better than that, but it ain't no fun gettin' caught in a cloudburst. Never know what can happen."

"You're right about that. We'll just keep an eye on the clouds and the other'n out for some cover. We'll be alright," assured Ezra, nodding to the trail. "Wolf's wonderin' what the hold-up is." The big black wolf was jumping back and forth, watching for a sign from Gabe so he could take off again.

Gabe looked at the wolf, back at Ezra, then with quick open-handed motion, the wolf spun around and took off like he was chasing his supper. Gabe gigged Ebony to the trail, and they strung out again, making for the lower trail that paralleled the Wind, but crossed over a few creeks and the Little Wind River that came from the foothills of the Wind River Mountains.

Once on the flats, the grassy valley floor made travel easy. With gramma, bunch grass, and Indian grass, the horses snatched mouthfuls as they stretched out. Ebony set a good pace and as the sun was hanging over their left shoulders, Gabe guessed they had made about ten miles since they left the canyon. With seven or eight miles coming from the canyon, they had done well. But he wanted to travel further by the moonlight, but it looked like the storm clouds were going to change his plans. As he surveyed the approaching clouds, a sudden flash of jagged lightning lanced from the underbelly of the blackest cloud and snapped its fiery tongue at its earth-bound target.

Just the flare of fire told Gabe the storm was closer than he first thought, but he counted and when the roll of thunder made it sound as if the heavens above were splitting open, he knew the storm was closer than made him comfortable. He waited for Ezra and Dove to join him, "That storm is less than five miles away, so we need to be for finding some cover! Seen anything?"

Ezra started to shake his head, but Dove said, "There, at the edge of that bluff," pointing to a bluff with a long slope that extended into the valley, "there is a cut before that point. There is a basin with trees there."

Ezra and Gabe both looked at her, frowning, then to one another. Ezra said, "Here," handing her the lead to the packhorse, "You take this'n, I'll take the travois. You lead the way!" He glanced at Gabe to see his friend nod, and the two switched lead lines and Dove took the lead.

It was just over a mile to the cut, but the wind was kicking up and the lightning was coming more frequent. The horses were getting skittish and the riders had to use a firm hand and some encouragement with words and touches, but they made the split beside the bluff and Dove led the way into the small basin. To the right, and nestled against the rising shoulder of the bluff, a cluster of juniper and cedar beckoned. As they neared, Gabe saw it was a camp that had been used before, there remained a fire ring of stones, three long poles that might have at one time been tipi poles that provided a makeshift three-sided corral, and the remains of a lean-to that sat between two of the larger juniper, whose lower branches had been trimmed away.

Gabe looked from Ezra to Dove and said, "Couldn't ask for a better camp than this!"

They quickly tethered the horses and stripped the gear, leaving the travois with the lodge and other packs on the lee side of the trees. They stacked the gear near the site of the lean-to and began stretching ground cover over the long pole and cutting branches to reinforce the covering. Dove was busy rolling out the blankets under the cover as the men finished the makings, intertwining the branches to shed the rain and resist the wind. Wolf lay beneath the cedar tree, watching and wondering if he was going to get to be in the shelter also.

Big drops of rain pelted them unexpectedly and each one hunched their shoulders and ducked under the edge of the trees, waiting for a sign from Dove that they could enter the lean-to, which came just before the worst of the storm. Both men dove for the entry and were pushed aside by Wolf, as he nestled down next to an already prone Dove. That put Gabe on one side and Ezra on the other, both men next to the cold ground sheet that served as the cover. But they were out of the rain and happy about it, so they took to the blankets but not before Dove passed out some jerky for their supper, even giving a handful to Wolf, who greedily gobbled his down.

The wind whistled through the trees as the big drops pelted the cover, sounding like a shower of hailstones rather that water, but there was nothing white about this storm. At least until a bolt of lightning cracked so close and with such force that everyone bounced off the ground with the impact, with both Wolf and Dove letting loose an exclamation of surprise. Gabe put an arm over Wolf's neck and asked, "What's the matter boy? You've been in storms before!" and chuckled at the wolf that scooted closer to him.

The rain continued well into the night, masking the sounds of anything else that might be happening in the nearby hills, yet the lean-to dwellers managed to slip off to sleep sometime after midnight. Only to be awakened by the combined whinnies of the horses and the bray of the mule. Gabe came up so fast his head hit the cover, shaking droplets of water onto his blankets and the others. "What's goin' on?" he asked of the darkness and crawled to the opening to push aside the hanging ends.

The roar of rushing water told him exactly what was happening, and he pushed out of the lean-to to stand and look around. The rain had let-up, but the cloud cover still mostly obscured the moon, and the darkness was so thick Gabe felt he had to push it aside to see. The roar of water was just below the camp and splashing past. He knew they had purposefully made their camp above the bottom of the draw, for this very reason, but now he was wondering if it was high enough.

He squinted and stepped away from the lean-to, feeling the presence of Ezra behind him as he spoke, "Comin' fast, risin' too. Gonna check to see how close." He moved forward, searching the shadows of the night, and saw the splashing of white water as it crashed over the rock-strewn gulch bottom. He looked uphill, saw the break in the hills that was the source of the flood water and turned back to Ezra, "Looks to me like it's gonna get even deeper. We better head up higher. You start with the woman and stuff; I'll saddle up the animals"

The men hustled around, wasting no movement nor time. Gabe wasn't concerned about riding, just about salvaging their gear and weapons. He saddled the horses quickly, put the packsaddles on the two pack animals, and was tying down the panniers when Ezra came to his side, arms full of ground covers and bedrolls. They tied everything down and the men lifted the heavy travois to the mustang, tied it off and Gabe motioned to Dove to lead the way up the slope to higher ground.

They chose to lead the horses and pick their way through the darkness. Everyone dug deep into the muddy hillside, feet and hooves making a mess of the shoulder of the bluff. Dove fell once, caught herself with her free arm and was back on the move. Ezra was leading his horse and the mustang with the travois, the heaviest load, and he had to do as much pulling as did the mustang, falling into the mud repeatedly as he tugged and pulled. Gabe brought up the rear, and had the worst of the trail to negotiate, and often did so with hands and feet at the same time.

It was a short distance to the top of the bluff and once there, Dove stopped, and sat down directly in front of her buckskin and tried to wipe some of the mud off as she listened to the groans and gripes from the two men and their animals. Wolf lay belly down beside Dove, looking back down the trail for the men, his tongue lolling out like he was laughing and Dove chuckled that the only thing about Wolf that was muddy was his paws.

As the men neared, she recognized Ezra, not by his usual appearance, but because he was shorter and a little broader than Gabe. But when Gabe came alongside and looked at Dove she said, "I know you two think you're brothers, but I never thought you looked like twins before, until now that is!" she declared, snickering as she said it, holding the back of her hand at her mouth.

They looked at each other, saw the resemblance, and both sat down in the mud beside their horses. Ezra looked at Gabe and asked, "Didn't we do all this to save ourselves, or was it just the gear?"

Gabe chuckled, "Musta been the gear, cuz we look worse'n we did when we started! Maybe we shoulda sat down in the stream and come clean, ya reckon?"

4 / CLEAN-UP

The storm had blown over and the moon smiled down on the dirty trio, offering them a way to the Little Wind River and some fresh water. Just over three miles to the northwest, the smaller river meandered down from the foothills, tracing its way past some clay buttes and ridges, before pushing southeast to join with its big brother, right after joining forces with the Popo Agie creek, to become a part of the Wind River. But here in the flats, the tall grasses waved a welcome to the group as they rode across the valley to the willow lined banks of the rambling stream.

Gabe led the way and as he approached, he glanced over his right shoulder to the first grey light then to the chuckling water and gigged Ebony right on into the water. The big black dropped his nose to the fresh water, drinking deep and long, and the mule pushed him further into the stream. Although no more than about thirty yards wide, the gravelly bottom showed beneath about two to three feet of clear water. Gabe swung his leg over the pommel and slid down the side of Ebony to splash into the fresh stream. Although the storm of the night had washed the gulches of the mountains with rainwater, most of the silt and debris had already washed past and downstream by the time they arrived at river's edge.

Gabe was sitting in the cold water, letting the current wash his duds and his body, as he let his arms dangle to the side. He cupped his hands and brought water to his face, but quickly saw the futility of that and ducked his head underwater, allowing the rushing stream to wash his hair, face and neck. He was stripping his tunic over his head when Ezra and Dove came to the riverbank, still mounted, and leaned over their pommels to watch the spectacle of the man in nature's pool. Wolf splashed in after him, jumped at Gabe and both went under but came up splashing and laughing.

Gabe looked at the others, "Dove, there's a backwater pool around the bend upstream there. If you wanna take that, I'll finish up here and Ezra can take my place. One of us'll be on watch all the while!"

"I'm not as muddy as you two, so I will not be long. You wash your duds while you are in there!" she instructed, grinning as she reined her buckskin beside Ezra to hand off the lead line to the mustang and the travois.

Gabe finished up, stripping down to bare nothin's and scrubbing his buckskins and underalls, before climbing out to fetch a blanket and his other set of buckskins. Ezra took his place in the water and before long, both men and animals were relieved of the nights mud and were ready for the days journey. Dove timidly joined them, showing off one of the new beaded tunics she had made just for the grand encampment. The golden buckskin was highlighted by the entire yoke beaded and quilled in a geometric pattern of diamonds and circles that spoke of the circle of life and her union with another that brought more life. Long fringe was capped with tufts of white rabbit fur, and her moccasins matched the dress with the beads and quills. The breast yoke was accented with a line of elk bugler teeth that dangled and bounced when she moved.

Ezra was spellbound as he looked at his beautiful woman and walked to her and the two embraced and spoke in hushed tones, sharing intimate thoughts and expressions of their love for one another. Gabe turned away and busied himself adjusting the packs and panniers on the mule and checking the loads of each of his weapons. He spoke over his shoulder, "If you two are through with your whisperin', maybe we could get back on the trail 'fore the encampment is over!" Ezra and Dove laughed, went to their horses and after checking their gear, mounted up to follow the over-eager leader of the group.

By late afternoon, after crossing some dry flats with nothing but sage and creosote brush and plenty of cacti, they came to the Wind River, crashing its way southeast through the wide valley that lay in the shadow of the mountains of the same name. The green of the valley bottom contrasted with the muted browns and greys of the lower foothills from both sides of the valley. But the giggling waters of the Wind River cheered the trio as it crashed over the rocks and twisted its way snake-like to work its way down the valley.

The brief stop at river's edge for the animals to drink, gave Gabe the opportunity to scan the hillsides. He stepped down, went to a pile of rocks and took out his scope for a better look. As he searched the terrain around, he saw deer, elk, antelope, coyotes, lots of jackrabbits, and a prairie dog village, but nothing that spoke of danger. He stood, looking toward the Wind River mountains, knowing this entire territory where they traveled was known to be the land of the Shoshone, but there were no boundaries, fences or hedgerows like in the white man's world. All land was subject to raids by both war parties and hunting parties from any tribe that chose to travel into this land. The nearest were the Crow, their land lying to the east and northeast, the Cheyenne, further east, and the Blackfoot to the north and northeast. Yet other bands like the Gros Ventre and the Sioux, with Hidatsa, Hunkpapa, Two Kettle and Oglala bands, have also been known to raid into Shoshone country. And to the southeast were the Arapaho. Gabe was thinking of all those tribes as he scanned the countryside, an area where they had a run-in with some Crow the last time they traveled this country.

They pushed on, stopped for a rest and a meal, then mounted up again to ride into the night. It was at Gabe's insistence they travel by moonlight for the next couple nights, or until they made the headwaters of the Wind River. The moon was waning from full and they would have two or three nights of ample light for their travels.

It was close to midnight on the second night of their trek that the moon shone bright on the pale clay foothills on their right. The valley bottom carried the river below them, as they rode the low shoulders of the timbered hills on their left. Hills that stood as black shadows and shouldered one another aside as they rode by, glancing from the shadows to the brightness of the long sloping hills on their right that stretched into the valley from the crests of the tail end of the craggy peaks of the Absaroka Range. Gabe motioned them to drop off the flat butte to the river below where they would give the horses a breather.

The valley had continually narrowed with foothills pushing in from both sides, and Gabe knew they were nearing the headwaters of the Wind River, but it would take at least another night's travel, maybe more, to reach the pass that would cross the mountains into the valley of many smokes. He found himself getting a little edgy, uncomfortable. He never liked confined spaces and they were nearing a cut between the hills marked by a stony point that pushed the river against the timbered hillside, forcing it to cascade over the rocky bottom where they would have to take to the water to make it through the cut. He knew they would be vulnerable at that point and he thought about their best tactic.

Ezra led his bay and the mule away from the water to join Gabe as he sat waiting, watching Ebony and the roan graze. Ezra had taken back the mule, letting Gabe have the roan, and Dove still led the mustang and travois. As Ezra approached, "You're a little antsy. What's wrong?"

"I dunno. Just the narrow valley I reckon. You know me, I like open spaces or at least somewhere I can see what's around me. That narrow cut up there puts us in the water and vulnerable."

Ezra turned to look at the shadowy cut, marked by the white stone of the point, and nodding his head, turned back to Gabe. "Ummhmm, so, what're we gonna do?"

Gabe thought a moment, then suggested, "How's 'bout you take the roan, tie the mule behind him, and lead 'em both. I'll go ahead, an' if it's clear, I'll give you a nighthawk call, and you come on."

"Simple 'nuff. We can do that."

Ezra took the lead of the roan from Gabe, draped it over his saddle as he moved the roan behind his bay. Then tying off the lead of the mule to the bay's tail, he nodded to Gabe, who had mounted up and waited. Gabe nodded back and started Ebony to the cut. Within moments they were splashing through the shallow waters, moving upstream on the left edge, crowding the bank that fell under the shadow of the white rock point. He held the Ferguson across his thighs, finger on the trigger, thumb on the hammer.

The clatter of hooves against rock and the splash of water was slightly masked by the cascades of the stream coming over the larger boulders that littered the stream bottom, but the sound was also magnified by the close confines and Gabe knew if there was anyone near, they would know something was coming up the creek. He had a quick thought that if there was anyone, maybe they would hesitate at the thought it could be elk. But he pushed on, around the point and into the shadows of the narrows.

The hill on the right lay back away and offered a bit of shoulder and a trail that beckoned Gabe from the water. The big black stepped up the low bank and eagerly took to the trail. But the taller and steeper timbered hillside on the left bank, stood dark and ominous as the stream rode the bottom rocks at its edge.

Just a little further and the valley opened wide on both sides, offering a clear moonlit view of an open vale. Gabe stood in his stirrups and twisted back toward the cut and lifted the cry of the nighthawk, the peent and boom at the end that carried in the night. Within moments, Gabe heard the clatter of hooves on rocks and Ezra and Dove soon came alongside. They nodded to one another, then Gabe spoke softly, "I don't like it."

"I know what you mean. My neck hair is standing up like a cornstalk!" answered Ezra.

Gabe looked back upstream, took a deep breath that lifted his shoulders, looked at Ezra, "Stay ready," and started off. As he moved away, Ezra slipped his rifle from the scabbard under his right leg, lay it across his thighs and with thumb on the hammer, started after his friend. Usually, they would travel until close to sunrise before making camp, but now it was uncertain. Something was out there, both men felt it, and neither was comfortable with stopping.

5 / COMPANY

"No! Not Wind River," declared Dove, pointing to the wider valley that led to the north. She pointed to a small cut and narrower valley that pointed to the northwest, "There!" The river that had been their guide hugged the foothills on the right and in the moonlight, appeared to come from the wider valley. But Gabe looked where Dove pointed, saw the shadows of tall trees, probably cottonwood, that made a line from north to south across the valley and appeared to twist around the shoulder of a small bluff that stood before them, dividing the two valleys.

Gabe looked from Dove to Ezra and back to the wide valley before them, "Alright, since you've been here before and I haven't, we try it your way." He gigged Ebony to cross the river beside them and took to the tall grass that painted the valley floor. On their left, timber covered hills stood sentinel like as imposing shadows that moved beside them, while the barren mesas on the east side of the valley shouldered up against the ragged pinnacles of the Absaroka Range that made the night sky resemble the torn hem of the heavens.

The creak of leather on the saddles, the slough of horses hooves parting the tall grass, the occasional snort of a horse, or even the groan of a rider, were sounds that were filtered out of Gabe's consciousness as he paid close attention to his surroundings. But try as he might, he heard no owl asking questions, no cry of a night hawk hunting his dinner, no howl of coyote or wolf, and no clatter of cicadas or grasshoppers. He reined up, motioned for Ezra to come close, and whispered, "Hear that?"

Ezra frowned, cocked his head, "Nothin'!"

Gabe slowly lifted his head in a nod, glanced down at his rifle still across his thighs, and cocked his head to the side to listen again. With the animals standing quiet, no one moving, still there was no sound, which could only mean something, or someone had alarmed the usual nocturnal creatures into stillness. Gabe's nostrils flared, and his forehead wrinkled in a frown, as he looked to Ezra to see the same reaction on his face. "Smoke!" he whispered.

They were in the open and exposed, even in the moonlight, but there was no cover nearby. Gabe motioned to the tree line beside the river at the base of a long bluff, the same bluff that pushed the narrow stream around its peninsula point. He started toward the trees, about a half-mile distant, it was that or take to the trees on the steep slope of the hill beside them, but not certain of where the smoke came from, he opted against the steep hill, preferring the better cover beside the stream.

They moved silently through the tall grass, Wolf making waves as he pointed the way before them. This was the Wind River, much smaller than before, no more than forty feet across and less than two feet deep. The moonlight showed an easy crossing and after seeing a good clearing between the bluff and the river on the far side, Gabe pushed on across. They reined up and stepped down, rifles in hand, quickly tethering the animals. Gabe whispered, "You and Dove make camp. I'm climbin' that ridge, going out on the point, to see if I can find that campfire we been smellin'." He lifted his eyes to the night sky, saw several stars winking their last glimmer of light, the moon resting on the rim of the western mountains, and the eastern sky beginning to lighten. "I'm takin' my scope, gonna search things out. I'll signal if'n I see anything, otherwise, I'll just come back for some fresh coffee!" he grinned as he slapped Ezra on his shoulder. But both men knew what was needed and as Dove set about making camp, Ezra searched the nearby trees, moving broken limbs and branches to serve as noise makers if anyone tried to approach.

Gabe and Wolf angled up the hill behind the camp, and once atop, went into a low crouch, then all fours as he crawled beside Wolf, who was belly down, to the point of the bluff. Gabe searched the riverbed directly opposite the point of the bluff where a narrow valley split the hills and a wide alluvial plain pushed into the valley. Beside the hill across the stream, lay a narrow creek bottom, a clearing alongside the creek, and the area surrounded by trees, cottonwood, juniper and aspen. *An ideal campsite,* thought Gabe, squinting his eyes to look for any smoke or movement, but saw none. With another extended search, he then began to scan up the river and the valley that carried the stream from its headwaters. Willows, aspen and some stunted cottonwood grew close to the water and twisted their way to follow the serpentine path of the narrow stream. But again, no movement nor smoke. He turned to scan the hills below the point, most were timber covered and dark, too dark to see anything.

Gabe lay still, listening, watching, as his nostrils flared to take in the mountain air and maybe give a hint as to the source of the smoke. And the hint of pine smoke filled his nostrils, making him think it had to come from nearby. Off his left shoulder, the sky began to pale, and shades of grey lined the eastern horizon, slowly turning lighter and showing blue. Shadows began to stretch and show themselves different from the land, and Gabe stared at the clearing below, slowly moving his eyes around the edge of the clearing. Then he saw a picket line of horses, just inside the tree line and he could make out four. Closer in, beneath the thicker juniper, he began to see movement. As he watched, one figure separated himself from the shadow of a tree near the horses and walked toward the others. Within moments, Gabe could make out four figures, obviously native, but in the dim light, he could not make out anything that would identify the people or tribe.

The four stood close together, talking and gesturing, the one that had been separate was pointing toward the river and the valley below. *He musta heard us in the dark but couldn't locate us. Now they're gonna hafta figger out what they oughta do about us,* thought Gabe as he watched. As the sun peeked above the hills to the left, Gabe slipped his scope from its case and stretched it out, shielding the end from the light to keep any reflection from showing. He focused in on the four, noticing the top knots, feathers, long hair on three, the long braids on one that had a knot of hair at the back that held three feathers. Their attire and hair suggested they were Shoshone, but who, what band, why were they here?

As he watched, the four gathered their gear and went to their horses to mount up. The one with braids led out and they started to follow the river as it bent around the point. Gabe came to his feet and in a crouch, staying just below the crest of the hill he ran back towards their camp. As he neared, he let loose with the chattering whistle of the Whiskey Jack, a warning of danger to Ezra. Then with the trees as cover, he and Wolf descended the hill at a run, and were soon in the cover of the trees. He came near the clearing and spoke from the trees, just loud enough for Ezra to hear, "Four warriors, maybe Shoshone, coming your way," and dropped back into the trees.

The four riders stayed away from the tree line, searching the grasses for sign of passage. Suddenly one reined up, motioned to the others and they came to his side. Without speaking, he pointed to the tracks, then toward the trees at the riverbank. Nothing showed on their side of the river, the trees were too scattered to shelter anyone, but those across the stream were thicker and could shield several. The warrior with braids motioned to the others and two went to the right, one stayed with the braids, and they moved to the left of the obvious place of crossing for whoever had come in the night.

As they came to the trees, they dismounted and waded into the cold water. The one with braids, obviously the leader, held a rifle across his chest, the one beside him had an arrow nocked in his bow. Those that were further downstream were both armed with bows, although one had a war club hanging at his back beside his quiver. They silently moved across the water, stepping up onto the bank and picking their way through the trees.

Ezra had gone to the tree line beside the river and watched the warriors approach. He went back to the camp and he and Dove, with rifles at hand, acted as if they were making camp and readying to make a meal. At the sound of buckskin brushing a branch, Ezra grabbed his rifle and in a crouch, watched as the first two showed themselves just inside the trees.

"A-ho!" shouted the one with braids. Then spoke in English, "We come in peace!"

Ezra slowly stood and Dove came from behind him, also holding a rifle, as Ezra spoke, "Come on in, then."

The two warriors, holding their weapons at the ready, slowly walked from the trees and into the camp. The leader frowned and looked at the two that stood before the fire ring, "You are Shoshone?" speaking in the language of the people and to Dove.

"We are both Shoshone," she answered. "This is my man, Black Buffalo, and I am Grey Dove of the *Kuccuntikka,* the band of Broken Lance."

The leader obviously relaxed, "I am *Doyakukubichi' Wa'ipi,* Cougar Woman, the war leader of the *Tukku-tikka,* the band of Little Weasel. This," nodding to her companion, "is Bull Hunter."

Both Ezra and Dove nodded at the introductions, then Ezra said, "You should call the other two in before my friend kills them."

Cougar frowned, eyes flared as she looked around, then called out, "Little Mountain, Snake Eater, come!"

Ezra whistled an answer to Gabe, the chattering whistle of the magpie, and heard the response. Then motioned to the two before him to be seated. He nodded to Dove and she kindled the fire, using the flint and steel on the already prepared tinder, and flames soon flared, and she stood back.

Ezra looked to Cougar Woman and asked, "Are your people going to the grand encampment?"

"Yes, we are scouting for our villagers, you?"

"The same."

"This other man, who?" she asked.

"Spirit Bear, my brother. He has been watching your camp and told us of your approach."

She smiled, glanced to the man beside her, then looked up to see the other warriors approaching through the trees. She motioned them in, then directed them to retrieve their horses. Both men trotted off and could be heard crossing the stream. Gabe had silently come into the clearing behind the visitors and spoke to Ezra, "Everything alright?"

His words startled the two visitors who jumped to their feet and turned to face Gabe as Ezra said, "Cougar Woman, Bull Hunter, this is Spirit Bear, also known as Gabe."

Gabe was surprised to hear the war leader referred to as woman, but his quick glance assured him she was definitely a woman, and a very beautiful one at that. Although her facial expression was one of surprise and even anger, the fire in her eyes betrayed her spirit and the long hair shone in the morning light as the iridescence of a raven's wing. Her tunic and leggings did little to hide her figure that was accented by the beading and fringe of the buckskins. The three feathers in the knot at the back of her head told of her prominence and experience as a war leader, each one notched and marked accordingly. She was tall, just a couple inches shorter than Gabe who stood six foot three inches, and stood proudly, shoulders back and head high as she looked upon the man that had come behind her so silently she was totally unaware and that had never happened.

She looked at the bear claw necklace that hung around Gabe's neck and at his beaded and fringed buckskins, and was pleased by what she saw, but did nothing to betray her judgment of the man. He was broad shouldered, and his stance told her he was a man to be respected. She turned away from him and sat down, then lifted her eyes to Dove and spoke to her, "You have two men for your lodge?"

Dove grinned, "No, Black Buffalo is my man and he is more than most women could have. Spirit Bear was married to my sister, who has crossed over."

Cougar Woman slowly lifted her head to acknowledge what was said, then turned to look at Gabe as he seated himself across the fire from her. "You move well through the trees. Never has a warrior done so like you to come behind me."

"You were busy with my brother, it was nothing."

At her first glance she had made note of his weapons, the rifle held close, the pistol in his belt, the tomahawk at his side. But she saw no knife or other weapons. And the one called Black Buffalo was also armed with pistol, rifle and tomahawk, but he also had a knife at his belt. The woman also had a rifle and knife. Cougar Woman looked around the camp, counted six animals, and a considerable stack of gear as well as a travois with a hide lodge.

Cougar looked at Gabe, "Are you traders?"

"We've done some, but we're not traders."

Wolf trotted into the camp, startling the visitors, but when he trotted to a cradle board was the first she noticed the baby. She leaned to the side to see the wolf and the baby and frowned, then realized that Gabe was watching her and grinning. She glared at him, "That wolf, he is with you?"

"Ummhmm, the baby too! The boy is called Chipmunk, and the wolf is just Wolf." Gabe grinned, then snapped his fingers and with a simple hand motion brought Wolf to his side. He stood, and with Wolf at his side walked to the woman who leaned back at their approach, but when Gabe went to one knee beside Wolf and had his arm around his neck, he said, "Wolf, this is Cougar Woman, she is a friend." Wolf looked from Gabe to the woman and took a tentative step toward her, lowering his head and looking up at her. She held out her hand for him to smell, then reached forward to touch the side of his head, looking from Wolf to Gabe with each move.

When Wolf allowed her touch, she relaxed and said to Gabe, "I have never touched a wolf and he is beautiful!"

Gabe grinned, stood and walked back to his seat, Wolf following. "I found him as a pup, just a few days old, and he's been with me since."

The strip steaks were sizzling over the flames and the biscuits were browning as the smell of coffee filled the air. The visitors did not have coffee cups and Gabe and company only had two spares, so the visitors shared, and all were pleased with the rare treat of fresh coffee. It was at Gabe's suggestion that they travel together, "Seein' as how we're goin' the same place for the same thing, makes sense to travel together, don't you think?"

Cougar Woman nodded, pleased at the suggestion. She had already thought she would like to get to know these people better, especially the big one called Spirit Bear. She brought the cup away from her lips, kept a stoic expression, "The bigger group would be easy to see, but," she paused, "It would also be safer with more warriors."

"Sound's like a good idea to me," added Ezra, giving a furtive grin to his wife as he winked, knowing they both were thinking the same thing about Gabe and Cougar Woman.

6 / CROSSING

The movement of the broad rear of the horse showed long strides but a smooth gait, not uncommon for a horse of that size. The palomino and white paint stood a little taller than Gabe's Ebony, at about fifteen three hands, and the woman that sat astride sat comfortably and confidently on the short-backed horse. Gabe watched the long slope with bunch grass and sage slide away toward the river, left of their trail, while on their right a tall knob of a barren hill separated the two valleys with the Wind River carving its way through the smaller of the two. A lower bald knob stood forlornly to the left, hiding the meandering course of the Wind as Cougar Woman led them on a well-used trail that rose over the saddle between the two buttes.

Gabe willingly yielded the lead to the war leader who had traveled this way before and confidently took the point. But Gabe signaled Wolf to scout and the big black wolf stretched out ahead of the group, roving at will, but watchful for anything and anyone. Gabe was confident in the Wolf and knew he would give ample warning of any danger. But Cougar Woman trusted no one but herself, having seen the fallacy of placing her confidence in another and choosing her own way, rather than placing her life in another's hands.

The Wind River, now not more than a creek, chattered its way along its descending course, as it carved its bed between the foothills that lay between the Wind River and Absaroka mountains. After a couple miles, the valley widened with a serrated slope of pale clay dropping from the ridge on their right, that lined the valley on the north side from a height of about eight hundred feet. While on the south side, a smattering of hills, knobs and ridges, all timber covered lay sloping away from the riverbed. About five miles along the trail, the river and valley took a dog-leg bend to the right and pointed to the north.

The trail was just above the valley floor and rode the skirt of a rimrock ridge that showed the crest of a mesa flat that lay between the rimrock and a line of foothills that pointed to some granite mountain top pinnacles further north. On their left stood a long basaltic ridge that looked like a wall above the black timber and rising about twenty-five hundred feet above the valley floor. At its crest, Gabe spotted what he thought to be an ancient volcano, which would explain the abundance of basaltic rock along the ridge and more.

The trail rode the face of the slope and slowly climbed above the riverbed. Gabe's first thought was this was the headwaters of the Wind River, but the round knob that stood as a barrier to the valley, shouldered the river around its point while the trail they were following appeared to bend to the right and rise higher on the shoulder of the towering mountain before them. Then Wolf came down the trail at a run and Gabe knew there was some danger ahead. Wolf ran past Cougar Woman, startling her horse and causing her to lift the reins taut, as she watched the wolf race past. Wolf came to a quick stop as he looked up at Gabe, turned to look up the trail, and dropped into his attack stance and let a growl rumble. Gabe glanced ahead, shouted, "Down!" and rolled to the left and off his horse, rifle in hand. He dropped to one knee, saw Cougar also on the ground, glanced back to see Ezra and Dove also down, but the other warriors, staggered between Dove and Ezra, were looking around, nocking arrows, looking for attackers. But their delay cost them, as an arrow pierced the neck of Bull Hunter, taking him to the ground, another cutting a path across the shoulder of Snake Eater, but the bigger warrior, Little Mountain hit the ground on his feet, looking over the back of his horse as he searched for a target.

Cougar called, "There!" motioning to the trees to the left of the trail, opposite the attack. She grabbed the reins of her mount and used it as a shield as she took to the trees below the trail. Gabe watched the hillside above, his rifle resting across the saddle as he searched for a target. He saw movement, then the shoulder of one man, and quickly drew a bead, just to the left of the shoulder, and squeezed off the shot, knowing the big bullet would penetrate the thin scrub oak the warrior used as cover. The Ferguson bucked and belched lead and smoke, and instantly the hidden warrior reared back and fell to the side, kicking and groaning, then lay still.

Gabe grabbed the reins and led Ebony from the trail at a long-legged trot, taking him behind a big juniper, loosely wrapping the rein around a branch as he snatched both pistols from the saddle holsters and stuffed them in his belt. He looked to the hillside, and began reloading the Ferguson by feel, rather than sight, watching the others of their group find shelter, and searching the hillside for another target.

He dropped to a crouch and worked his way nearer Cougar Woman, who was behind a rock outcropping that held a scraggly piñon that clung to a crack in the large boulder. Her rifle lay along the stone, and she stood quiet, watching. Gabe had dropped to one knee nearer the juniper to the right of the rocks, but within about ten feet of Cougar Woman. "Can you tell who they are?" he asked.

"Blackfoot!" she snarled. "*Piikani!*" she spat the word that identified the band of Blackfeet as the Piegan, the largest of the tribes of the Blackfoot confederacy.

Gabe watched the hillside, trying to determine how many attackers they faced, and made the best count possible, looked to Cougar, "Looks like about twelve. That what you figger?" he asked.

Without looking his way, "More than two hands, maybe three."

Gabe had looked around at their position, and although it wasn't the worst spot he had been in, it wasn't the type of cover he preferred. He looked to Cougar again, "I'm gonna check on the others. I'll be right back."

He moved back from the big Juniper and started back along the line where the others had taken cover. He passed Little Mountain, shook his head at the name of such a big man, nodded as he passed and noted the man was unhurt. A short distance further, he saw Snake Eater, his back bloody, but not too bad, and nodded as he moved past. Dove was hunkered behind another big boulder, rifle in hand, but not showing herself as a target. She looked at Gabe as he came near and Gabe encouraged her, "Keep down, we'll take care of these." She nodded, and Gabe moved past to where Ezra stood behind a thick trunked cedar, his rifle resting on a branch as he searched for a target.

He turned to Gabe as he neared, "What're they doin'? Ain't been any shootin' or anything since that first volley."

"I think they're wantin' to work a little closer. Near as I can tell, where they're hunkered, it's a bit of a long shot for their bows. I think they expected to get us all with that first barrage, and if Wolf hadn't come runnin', they probably would have got most of us. I took one out 'fore I took to the trees, but I think there's about a dozen more. They're Blackfoot."

Ezra looked back at Gabe at the word, and spat, "Blackfoot! That's all we need. Them boys don't give up easy!"

"Uhnuh, they sure don't. So, I'm thinkin' we might have to do somethin'."

"Now, that's an understatement. We sure can't sit here an' wait for them to do somethin'," answered Ezra. "But, I'm not sure I want to hear what you want to do." He turned away to look at the mountainside and watch for any movement or target.

"I think I might be able to work around this end and come down on 'em from above. But I need you to go tell Cougar not to shoot me! Them others, too!"

"And just what else do you want me to do, charge 'em from here?" asked Ezra as he shook his head at the suggestion of his friend.

Gabe couldn't help but chuckle a little as he looked at Ezra, "No, but give me, oh, ten minutes, if they wait that long, and then start takin' some potshots at 'em to keep their attention thisaway."

"Oh, so that's it. You want me to be a target for them, so you won't!" jibed Ezra, turning back to look at Gabe.

Gabe let a grin split his face, then checked the loads on all three pistols that weighted down his belt, then re-checked the rifle, felt his possibles pouch and touched the tomahawk. Then with a nod, moved away from his friend to work below the slope before cutting across the trail and moving above the attackers.

It took all of the ten minutes, but the silent stalker moved quickly and quietly, making certain to not allow his buckskins to brush against any branches or thicket of scrub oak, and picking every step to avoid loose stones, twigs, dry leaves, or anything that could make noise and give him away. He was above and behind the Blackfoot, and counted thirteen, plus the one dead one that lay sprawled where he fell. He was a little more than thirty feet above them, close enough to be accurate with the pistols and he slipped the Bailes over/under from his belt. The two French pistols were bigger, faster and with longer barrels, more accurate at a distance. He would save them for later shots. He looked along the jagged row of shooters, wondered why they had not attacked, then saw the man on his far left rise a little, looking back at his warriors and start to lift a hand to signal the others.

Gabe brought up his rifle, bringing the hammer to full cock as he tried to mask the sound behind the brush before him, and just as the man started to stand to shout and signal, Gabe pulled the trigger and started the battle. The Ferguson roared and the bullet struck true, but Gabe did not wait to see what he knew was a hit. He lifted the Bailes, cocking the hammer and drawing a bead on a closer warrior, just as he heard the rifles of Ezra and Cougar sound as one racketing roar. He dropped the hammer and the bullet blossomed red in the neck of the nearest warrior below him. He quickly rotated the barrels of the Bailes, picking his next target and saw the warriors moving about, realizing someone was behind them, and when a Blackfoot turned and lifted his rifle toward Gabe, the second barrel roared and the man was knocked back into the brush behind him.

Gabe quickly dropped the Bailes, and pulled the first of the two saddle pistols, cocking the first hammer, and choosing another target. The French pistol bucked in his hand and the smoke obscured his target, but Gabe didn't hesitate to bring the second hammer to full cock as he looked for another warrior. He snapped off another shot, but he was a little hasty as he did and the warrior flinched, evidently not seriously hit, and stood to his feet to bring his bow to full draw just as Gabe grabbed for the second saddle pistol. As his fingers wrapped around the grip, he glanced to see the bow shooter arch his back and red blossom on his chest as Ezra's bullet found its mark. The arrow was loosed and flew wildly into the brush.

Gabe twisted around, searching for a target, but the rest of the warriors had found cover and were not easily found. Gabe grabbed the Ferguson and started reloading. He spun the trigger guard to open the breech, placed the wadded ball in the breech, filled it with powder and spun the trigger guard to cut off the load to the right amount and close the breech. He slapped open the frizzen, filled the pan, snapped it shut and lifted the rifle to his shoulder as he searched for another target. He stuffed the two empty pistols in his belt beside the second saddle pistol, and in a crouch, sought another vantage point.

As he moved, he heard the sporadic rifle fire from below, the occasional rifle fire from the Blackfoot as they returned fire against the others and heard the rattle of arrows clattering to the brush and rocks without finding their target. He moved to the edge of a scrawny piñon, saw a sprawled Blackfoot, an arrow in his chest but still struggling to move. From his new position, he spotted three others, one to his far left, two closer below. He pulled the loaded pistol from his belt, lay it beside him, and slowly lifted his rifle to his shoulder.

As he brought the sights down on the far warrior, he eared the hammer back, slipped his finger to the forward trigger, and slowly squeezed. The big rifle responded with a roar as it spat death to drop the far warrior, and before the smoke cleared, Gabe had lifted the pistol and taken aim at a startled warrior below and to his right. The man turned to look at Gabe, eyes wide and fear showing, but he lifted his bow just as the pistol roared and ended his life as the bullet pierced his sternum and shattered his backbone. Gabe quickly looked to his next target and snapped off his second shot, the bullet ripping through the warrior's shoulder and taking him to the ground, writhing in pain as he grabbed at his wound that spurted blood.

Gabe retreated behind a sizable boulder and began to reload his weapons, peeking over the edge often to see what the others were doing. But he could see little, as he frantically sought to load all his weapons. The Ferguson was first and sat beside him, ready. The Bailes was in his belt, both barrels loaded. The first saddle pistol lay on the stone beside him, also loaded and he looked around the boulder for another quick search of the brush below. Still he saw nothing. He finished loading the last of his pistols, stuffed the two saddle pistols behind his belt and picked up the Ferguson. He moved to the other side of the stone, and cautiously looked around, searching for the Blackfoot, but nothing moved. The rifle fire from below had stopped, and none of the remaining Blackfoot were moving. Gabe waited, watching, and after a few moments, he heard from far up the valley, the sound of horses retreating at a run.

He searched the brush again, stepped out to wave at Ezra and the others, then carefully worked his way through the brush, checking each of the downed warriors for signs of life. He saw that the man with the torn shoulder had apparently bled out and lay lifeless beside the brush. All the others, including two that had taken arrows, were dead. Typically, he didn't count the number, but knew all but one of his shots had scored a kill.

As he walked to the others, they came from their cover and led the horses back to the trail. No one spoke until Ezra looked at Gabe, "So, what took you so long? You said ten minutes, but it was longer'n that!"

"Hey, next time I'll sit back and watch and let you climb the mountain!" answered Gabe as he drew near. Cougar Woman watched him walk up to Ebony, she had led him along with her paint from the trees, and as Gabe took the reins, she looked at the pistols in his belt, frowned, "I thought I would hear two or three shots, but . . ." she paused as she looked. "Are they all down?" referring to the Blackfoot.

"No, some of 'em snuck off while I was reloadin', but they're long gone."

"How many dead," she asked, nodding to the brush on the hillside.

"All of 'em," he answered, stoically, as he swung back aboard the big stallion.

7 / MEAT

Cougar Woman led off as the group took to the trail that pointed to the top of the pass. The trail split two peaks, the one on the left showing granite talus slopes while the one on the right stood majestically still clinging to glaciers in the narrow clefts. Jagged edged limestone cliffs scarred the face of the steep mountain, rising to form a hogback ridge that appeared as a stony curtain on the north wall of the valley. The headwaters of the Wind River were no more than a trickle of spring fed and snow melt waters. This late in the warm months, most of the snow had served its purpose and had already passed below as cold mountain runoff, feeding the myriad of streams that joined to form the mighty rivers.

Cougar led them through the black timber that crowded the narrow trail, breaking into a wide patch of aspen that shook their leaves at the passersby. Gabe breathed deep of the thin mountain air, feeling alive with the cool temps and the clear air and the majestic mountain scenery. He looked at the back of Cougar Woman, at one with her mount, her movements an extension of the horse's, her head held proudly high as she obviously was also enjoying the mountain trail.

The scent of pine and cedar blended with the soft touch of the columbine and lupine, reminding Gabe of the many times he and Otter had reveled in the joys of the mountains. But his glance to Cougar Woman took his thoughts in a different direction. She was a beautiful woman, a strange blend of beauty and courage, a war leader for her people, an honor not easily earned. But she was not masculine, everything about her spoke of femininity and beauty, but a war leader had to have daring and courage as well as wisdom and strength, and these she had shown. *She's a woman to stand beside a man and make him proud, not as a decoration or someone to serve him, but one that would be an equal.* His thoughts surprised him for he had not thought of another woman in that way since his first meeting with Pale Otter, but the two women were very different, each special and beautiful, but also unique. *But a woman like that probably already has a mate, probably a chief or other leader,* he thought, forcing his mind to other things.

As they crested the trail between the peaks, a wide valley opened before them. Although mostly tundra and bog, the graze had attracted a herd of elk numbering about thirty. Some young bulls were at the far edge, growing antlers still in the velvet, but there were mostly cows and calves. The herd was strung out between the trail and south into a basin of grass with a few mounds of basaltic rock.

Cougar Woman reined up, waiting for Gabe to come near and as he approached, "Do we need meat?" she asked.

"We could use some, and I told our leader Broken Lance, we would leave some meat hanging for them as they followed."

"Why? Do they not have hunters?" queried the woman.

"Yes, but it would save time if we hung some in the trees for them. Would you prefer to keep going? If so, I can catch up later."

"We will wait," answered Cougar Woman, swinging a leg over the rump of her horse and sliding to the ground. She motioned to the others that they were stopping, and Gabe also stepped down, glancing back at Ezra and Dove. He slipped his sheathed Mongol bow from under the left fender leather of his saddle, reached across and lifted the quiver from the opposite side, and went to a nearby rock and began to string his bow.

Cougar Woman frowned, "What are you doing? You said you would take an elk, but . . ." she motioned to his case and quiver that sat beside his leg.

"Ummhmm, I am," he answered, and opened the case to withdraw the unusual looking weapon. "I figger to use my bow, not spook the rest of the herd or let any other Blackfoot know we're around."

He slipped the bowstring loop over the nock at one end, sliding the looped string down the limb a little, then placed his feet on the risers on either side of the hand grip. He began to bend the limbs back toward his hips. As he did he slipped the one loop into the nock, and deftly worked the other loop over the other nock, and slowly released the limbs to stretch the string taut.

Cougar Woman watched spellbound as this strange white man manipulated the unusual configuration of a bow from what did not resemble anything she knew as such a weapon, to one that was bent in odd ways. She watched silently, until he rose and started toward the tree line near the elk herd and when he motioned for her to come with him, she eagerly followed.

Ezra and the others had loosened the girths on the animals and found a comfortable place to sit as Dove handed out handfuls of pemmican. Ezra found some grass that grew in the shade of a couple of aspen and stretched out on the carpet of grass and leaves, where Dove soon joined him. He knew Gabe well enough to know that he would probably down at least two elk, maybe more, and then the work would begin for them all, what with field dressing and more. So, he was determined to get a little rest while he could and Dove gladly cuddled up next to him for the same reason.

Gabe took to the trees, following a bit of ridge that shadowed the basin where the elk grazed. Under the cover of the high-country fir and spruce, they used the carpet of needles to mask their stalk and soon came to the spot Gabe had chosen. At the edge of the trees was a cluster of kinnikinnick and as they neared the dark green brush, Gabe stopped, rose slowly to look over the herd. He nodded at the group nearby, "There's a cow without a calf, and that young bull," whispered Gabe.

Cougar looked where he indicated, saw the animals about seventy yards off and looked back at Gabe, "We must get closer," and turned away to return to the trees, but Gabe did not move and she stopped, waiting, watching.

Gabe stood tall, nocked an arrow and slowly started his draw. Cougar Woman frowned at his movement, noticing the way he held the string with his thumb on the string and fingers wrapped over the thumb, and shook her head at the actions of the man. But Gabe continued his draw and when the arrow was at a full-length draw, he released it and instantly reached for another arrow. His movements were swift, and the second draw was quicker, and the arrow released almost the same instant as the first arrow found its mark. Gabe had chosen the cow for the first target and the arrow flew true, burying itself to the fletching in the lower right chest of the cow who stumbled a step, tried another, and fell forward, neck stretched out as her legs gave way and she dropped to the ground.

When the young bull heard the strike of the arrow to the cow, he turned his head toward her, but before he took a step, the second arrow struck his lower left chest, driving through to impale itself in the right shoulder muscle. The bull's head came up, he stumbled forward, and staggered two steps before falling on his chin and rolling to his side, dead.

Cougar Woman's eyes flared wide, as she saw both elk downed. She turned to look at Gabe who had started for the elk, and she followed, walking in an ambiguous cloud of wonder at the feat she just witnessed. Not only had this man sent arrows such a distance, but he took two elk that were standing, facing each other, and before the second could move, he was downed. She had never seen the like and she was amazed at what she had observed. She stumbled after him, feeling somewhat insignificant. After witnessing what he had done against the Blackfoot, and now to take two elk with a bow, this man was more of a warrior and hunter than she had ever known. She looked at his back as he walked toward the downed elk, *and he is pleasing to look at also,* she thought, then shook her head to chase those thoughts from her mind.

Gabe knelt beside the cow, slipped his knife from the scabbard at his back, and cut her throat to bleed out. He stepped to the bull and repeated the move, wiped the blade on the hair of the bull and stood, slipping the knife into the sheath suspended between his shoulder blades, and looked at Cougar Woman. She had been silent since they stopped at the edge of the trees, and now she stood, looking at him, but he just grinned, looked back toward the aspen grove where the others waited, and with fingers to his mouth he let out a shrill whistle that mimicked the scree of a circling eagle. Within a short moment, Ezra stepped to the edge of the trees, waved, and they started into the basin, leading the horses of Gabe and Cougar.

Gabe lay the bow on a nearby boulder, put the quiver beside it, and extracted his knife again and taking a whetstone from his possibles pouch, leaned back against the boulder and began to sharpen the blade. Cougar also stood beside the boulder, leaned against it as she looked at Gabe and asked, "That bow," nodding toward the weapon atop the rock, "is different. Did you make it?"

"No, my father brought that home from one of his trips across the ocean," he looked up at her to see if she understood, but at her frown, "the big waters, where there are many countries far away. My father had traveled there and brought that back. It is a type used by a tribe known as Mongols. They have made that style of bow for many generations. It is called a Mongol Bow, it is made of laminated wood, ram's horn, sinew, and covered with birch bark." Cougar

Woman slowly lifted her head in a nod, but it was evident she did not understand.

"I have never seen anyone shoot an arrow to kill an elk at such a distance," she offered.

Gabe smiled, still working the blade on the whetstone. He spat on the stone, used the blade to move it about and into the stone, and continued his circular movements with the knife. He sighed heavily, then looked at Cougar Woman, "With that bow, I can shoot an arrow many times that distance." He looked back toward the trail where they had been and continued, "If there were an enemy on the trail yonder," nodding to the hillside, "I could kill him with one arrow." The trail was just shy of three hundred yards away, and he looked to Cougar Woman to see her response.

She frowned, looked at Gabe, shook her head and said, "No one can shoot an arrow that far!"

Gabe answered, "If I do, you will have to run and fetch it back. It is hard to make these arrows," he nodded to the quiver that held the black arrows.

"Ha! You cannot. If the arrow falls short, you will have to run and get it and I will shoot your bow and arrows while you run!" she laughed as she pictured him running away, trying to dodge her arrows.

But before the demonstration could begin, the others rode up, stepped down and came to their side as Ezra said, "So, how many didja get?"

Gabe nodded toward the two carcasses, noticing

the rest of the herd had moved further up the basin but still grazed. "Just two, that cow and young bull."

Ezra turned to Dove, "Guess we better get busy." He nodded to Gabe, "You an' Cougar can take Snake Eater and do the cow, while me'n Dove take Little Mountain and do the bull."

Ezra's assignment of duties precluded the archery contest, so everyone stepped to their tasks, chattering all the while and becoming better acquainted with one another. Cougar admitted to being the daughter of the village chief, Little Weasel, and that she did not have a mate. "I have considered it, but most have no interest in being the mate of a war leader, they are . . ." she paused, searching for the right expression, "afraid. But I have not found anyone suitable. I could not have a mate that could not match my skills in battle nor hunting, or even be better. But if they were better, then they would be war leader." She tossed a scrap of fat and gristle to Wolf who had busied himself at the gut pile, but quickly snatched up the offering.

Snake Eater was listening to the conversation, sneaking an occasional glimpse at Gabe, which he noticed, and never looking at Cougar. Then Gabe turned to Snake Eater, "Do you have a family?"

The warrior smiled, paused in his skinning, and looked to Gabe, "I have a fine woman, Rabbit Runner, and two," he held up two fingers, "fine sons. But they are small," he held out his hands to show one as a babe in arms and the other as a toddler.

Cougar Woman said, "His woman is a good friend, and a good mother."

Gabe looked at Snake Eater, "And I'm sure you will be a good father to your sons, take them hunting and more."

The man grinned, nodded, and resumed his work.

They deboned the meat, hung a big bundle in the hide of one from a tall branch of a spruce, made a rock cairn near the trail to point to the bundle for the followers, and strapped the other meat aboard a packhorse and took to the trail again. Wolf was hesitant to leave the offal to the carrion eaters, but neither would he be left behind and readily took the point to lead the way into the dim light of dusk. The sun was cradled on the western horizon, but they wanted to put some more miles behind them before they made camp for the night.

8 / SPECTACLE

At the base of the meadow near the trail, two small streams converged to join forces and push their way through the boggy flats and on into the mountain valley below. Both the trail and the streams hugged the timbered shoulder that lay below a long wall of limestone cliffs that stood as a formation of stiff grey soldiers standing sentinel over the green valley below. They paraded to the west rising and falling with the granite peaks, until the ridge of mountains dropped off and ended at a black timbered saddle that offered a pathway to a hammock of a valley that pointed to the north.

They had camped on the lee side of the saddle crossing amidst the black timber and rose early to take the trail into the next valley. From their promontory at the crossing, Gabe looked to the west to see the line of granite crags that stood as two opposing peaks, forming a barrier to anyone or anything that dared to cross from the low valley and over the Snake River to the green valleys at their back. He looked back to the north and leaned back in his saddle as they started the winding descent of the steep slope. At the bottom, they crossed over a shallow but broad creek, just above its confluence with another. They mounted a broad mesa that held scattered juniper and ponderosa. Another mountain rose to their right, east of the trail, it stood with heavy shoulders of granite, but at the far end, long spurs stretched between runoff made gullies to reach into the edge of the greener valley.

It was beautiful country and the type that made men like Gabe and Ezra happy to be alive and wandering in the wilderness. Cool air drifted down from the mountain peaks where pockets of snow and ice found refuge. The pines, cedars, spruce and more filled the air with their pungent fragrance, blending with the customary odors of men, horses, leather and the faint touch of gun smoke. The creak of saddle leather, the clatter of hooves on the trail, the whistle of a yellow-bellied marmot, and the scree of an over-head eagle, added to the enjoyment of the morning.

By mid-day, they were ready to leave the circuitous creek they followed to mount another saddle crossing to the north, but the horses needed a breather before starting another climb and the shallow but clear creek offered a refreshing drink. Cougar Woman signaled a stop, reined up and stepped down. The shoulder and mountain before them were littered with the remains of a fire that decimated the north slope some time ago. Now most of the downed trees were weathered and grey, with charcoal burn scars on the underneath sides. It was not an unusual sight, but even though new shoots and sprigs were pushing up green crowned heads, it was a somber reckoning of the danger of lightning storms in the mountains.

Ezra had gathered a bundle of dry limbs and twigs, dropped them in a pile and went down on his knees to start a fire, he glanced at Gabe, "Coffee, been hankerin' for some since we pulled out so early this mornin'. Didn't get muh usual two, three cups," he explained.

Gabe nodded, "While you do that, I think I'll climb that hill," nodding to the one behind him to the west of where they stopped, "and have a look-see. Save me some coffee, though."

"Will do, but don't take too long, I might get extra thirsty!"

Gabe slipped the cased scope from his saddle bags and started toward the butte, saw Cougar Woman frowning at him, waved her to join him and she came quickly to his side. She asked, "What you do?"

"Just gonna look around a little. Always like to see as much of the territory as possible, get a better idea of where we are, see if there's anybody ahead or behind us, you know, just scoutin'."

Wolf led the way as they angled across the face of

the butte, cut back and worked their way to the top of the bald dome. Gabe sat down, pulled the scope from its case and stretched it out as he pulled his knees up to use as a rest for his elbows and the scope. Cougar had sat down beside him, but about three, four feet away, watching.

When he lifted the scope to his eye and began scanning the far valley, she asked, "What is that?" nodding toward the scope.

Gabe brought it down, held it toward her and explained, "This has some special glass, like a clear rock, here and here," pointing to the ends, "but when you look through it, and adjust it, you can see further and clearer." He watched her reaction, saw confusion written on her face, and demonstrated for her by explaining as he lifted it to his eye, and adjusted it for clarity. He handed it to her and said, "Try it."

As she looked through it, she jerked back and looked in the direction she had looked using the scope, brought it back to her eye and held it. She slowly moved it side to side, looking at the distant mountains and valleys. She lowered it, looking at the brass tube, then lifted her eyes to Gabe, "It is . . ." and shook her head at the lack of description.

Gabe smiled as he took the scope from her and began scanning the area before them. "That sure is beautiful country! Plenty of game, there's moose, elk, oh, and a grizzly, he's a big 'un too!"

He lowered the scope, looked at Cougar, "Wanna see?"

She smiled and nodded, then he pointed to the distant valley, not more than three miles away, "He's sittin' in a berry patch, next to those willows by that little creek, just below them rocks!"

She nodded, lifted the scope and searched for the bear, focused the scope and leaned forward as she smiled. After a moment, she lowered the scope, looked to Gabe and said, "That is a wonder," nodding to the looking glass as she returned it to Gabe.

He smiled, "Guess we'll have to keep a look-out for that grizz when we get there." He stood, offered his hand for her to rise, and they started back down the trail, Wolf again in the lead. Cougar followed Gabe and Wolf down the trail, her mind working as she thought of the many ways this man had surprised her since the first time they met. With an ability to move through the woods that excelled anyone she knew, guns that shot many times, a shoots far bow, and now this scope as he calls it, that helps him to see far away. If he were a part of a tribe, he would be the chief or war leader. She watched him move, sure footed, down the rocky and steep trail, following his wolf friend, and that was amazing for a man to have a wolf for a friend. She shook her head in wonder and looked up as they came near the small cook fire that had the coffee pot dancing at the side and the smell of coffee in the air.

The horses and mule were tethered on the grass, Ezra sat beside the fire on one of the many downed logs, Dove was digging some smoked meat and pemmican from a pannier, and Cougar's two warriors were seated in the shade of a ponderosa, munching on strips of smoked meat. They looked at Gabe and Cougar as they came near the fire, Little Mountain said something to Snake Eater and they both scowled at Gabe, then returned to their meat.

Ezra reached for two more cups, poured them full of coffee and handed them to Cougar and Gabe as they sat, Gabe on the log with Ezra, Cougar on a log opposite where Dove joined her. Ezra looked at the women, "So, ladies, how much further to this grand encampment site?"

Dove looked to Cougar with a slight nod for her to answer and Cougar leaned forward slightly, "Three, four days. We will be close to the river that feeds the Lake of the Yellowstone before we stop this night. Then we will soon be beside that lake. Two, three days, we will be by the lake then take the water to the wide basin where the encampment will be beside the Yellowstone River."

Ezra nodded, then frowned, "You know, I never did know how that river got its name, do you know?"

Cougar frowned at Ezra, shook her head slightly as she looked at Dove and back to Ezra, "Because of the yellow stone," she replied, with an expression that told of her wonder that he should ask such a question.

"I figgered that, but I ain't seen no yellow stone anywhere along that river!" he explained.

Cougar nodded her head, understanding, "You will."

Ezra nodded, pursed his lips as he looked at Gabe and back at Cougar, then lifted his coffee cup to take a long draught. He poured a refill and blew on it, sipped a little, and breathed deep. Gabe knew he was working at containing his frustration and stifling his sassy words for a comeback, and hoped he succeeded. The last thing they needed was a division among their group. The attack by the Blackfoot spoke to that, for if they had been jumped when there was just the three of them, the outcome could have been much worse.

***

The trail rose over the rocky and broad saddle crossing that rode in the shadow of a large granite faced mountain that sat imposingly on the north of the trail, with heavy shoulders holding an exposed layer of limestone that had crumbled over the eons of time, dropping huge boulders to slide and roll to the valley floor. They followed a dry creek bed that had been carved by winter's runoff and forced its way through the fallen timber that had once stood at a black blanket covering the hillsides, but now lay as silent monuments, fading and disintegrating from mountainous ravages and time.

They broke into a wide flat-bottomed valley, small creeks chuckling their way over the rocks and gravel, offering the fresh water to the migrating herds of elk that passed. Cougar led them across the valley toward the mouth of a wide ravine that carried a runoff stream from the mountain tops. A wide swath of spruce and fir showed dark against the slope and the snow that still lingered in the shadows, and it was at the base of these tall trees that Cougar chose the camp for the night.

They stripped the gear from the horses, staked them out on the grass near the stream, then laid out their camp. The two warriors stayed near one another and rolled out their blankets uphill from the fire, Ezra and Dove were together at the edge of the trees beside the fire, and Cougar made her bed between Dove and her warriors, separating herself by about ten feet from either. Gabe took a solitary spot at the west edge for him and Wolf, between a pair of fir trees with their low hanging branches.

It was the beginning of dusk when they finished their supper, and Cougar spoke to Gabe, "Come with me, I want to show you a wonder of the mountains," then turning to Ezra and Dove, "You come as well." She stood and started into the trees, near the cascading stream that tumbled from the mountains and cut its path to the west of their camp. The trail she chose wound through the timber, and steadily climbed. After about two hundred yards, Gabe cocked his head to the side, looked at Cougar and asked, "Are there two streams? It sounds like there's another over there," nodding to their right, east of their point.

Cougar smiled, nodded, "Yes, there are two. I will show you."

They climbed another fifty, sixty yards and came to the point where the two streams divided, having originally been one stream that carried the snow melt from on high. It appeared as if the two streams were the same size, the feeder stream dividing equally, and each creek headed down the slope of the alluvial mound, going its own direction. The group paused, looking from one stream to the other: neither more than four feet across, both cascading over the rocks and chuckling on their way. Gabe asked, "So, what's so unusual about a stream having a fork in it?"

Cougar smiled, "These two never join. This one," pointing to the easternmost creek, "goes down the mountain toward the rising sun to join the Yellowstone. That one," pointing to the other, "goes down the mountain that way, toward the setting sun, and joins the Snake River."

Gabe looked at the waters, then to Ezra, "That means that this one," pointing to the stream on his left, "flows to the Pacific ocean, and that one," nodding to the one on his right, "flows to the Atlantic." He turned around to look down the slope to the valley below,

"That means we are standing on the Great Divide!"

"Well, anyway you look at it, it's quite a spectacle. One foot on one side, and one on the other," answered Ezra.

The women looked at the men, frowning, not understanding. Neither had seen an ocean and thought little about the existence of such a thing, but they knew the men had been many places and were willing to accept the wonders of their ways, strange though they may be.

9 / THREATS

Little Mountain had hardly spoken to anyone but Snake Eater and Cougar Woman. The big man always wore a stoic expression and bulled his way about, stepping aside for no one and doing little more than tend to his own animal and that of Cougar Woman. When Gabe came from the mountain after his usual time with the Lord, he started toward the log where Cougar Woman sat, but Little Mountain sat beside her before he could get there. Gabe made a slight shrug, turned to pick up the coffee pot and poured himself some, looked to Cougar Woman and with a nod and raised eyebrows asked if she wanted some, but she glanced to Little Mountain and did not look back toward Gabe.

Gabe sat down on the log opposite Cougar Woman, accepted a tin with fried pork belly and corn pone from Dove, and looked to his eating. Ezra sat beside him, also working on his food, and asked, in low tones, "So, she leadin' us again today?" and took a sip of coffee.

"Reckon."

"Dove said it's just a matter of followin' this valley to the Yellowstone River, then follow that to the lake and the meetin' place is just beyond the lake. Sounds simple 'nuff to me."

"Prob'ly. But, since we been travelin' together, no reason to split off now, is there?" asked Gabe as he stuffed a corn pone biscuit in his chops.

"No, s'pose not. But, I don't know if you been noticin', that there Little Mountain don't seem to like you none. I'm thinkin' he has plans for Cougar Woman his own self," suggested Ezra.

"Could be. Didn't seem so cantankerous till this mornin'. I did see him and Snake Eater talkin' and lookin' at us like they were not happy with us being together," surmised Gabe, taking a big swig of coffee to cover his face with the cup as he spoke.

"Well, just watch things a little close, an' don't crowd 'em none. It's bad 'nuff fightin' off the Blackfoot, without tryin' to fight that mountain of a man."

Gabe let a bit of a grin tug at one corner of his mouth as he glanced to Ezra and stood to go to the horses and start rigging them for the day's travel. The well-practiced routine was quickly finished, Gabe rigging the roan and Ebony, Ezra tending to his horse, Dove's, the mule and mustang packhorse with the travois. Dove finished with the cookware and tins and cups, packed them in the pannier on the mule and was ready to mount up, when Cougar Woman and Little Mountain led off, without a backward glance to the others. As Gabe swung aboard Ebony, Snake Eater started after Cougar Woman and Little Mountain, giving a defiant glare over his shoulder as he passed Gabe.

Gabe frowned, concerned about the change of attitude with the two Shoshone Warriors and Cougar Woman's compliant manner with the two men. She was the war leader of their village and the two men were of no stature other than respected warriors. Gabe thought about their actions, considering the purpose or cause, whether it was the attitude of a jealous suitor or the protective moves of defenders concerned for their leader. He shook his head slightly, shrugged, and gigged Ebony on to follow the three, Wolf at his side.

They moved across the valley to take the trail on the east edge that followed the timbered spurs of the finger ridges that sloped into the valley from the higher mountains that were still clinging to the summer glaciers. After just two miles, Gabe's attention was captured by a wide valley that appeared to have been scooped out between two granite topped mountains, pointing back to the south before making a wide bend back east and carried a little snow-melt creek from high above. Another mile or so brought them to the confluence of four valleys and streams that joined the Yellowstone to promote it from a stream to a river. In the midst of the confluence rose a rim rock crowned butte that stood commandingly like a guard shack before a conglomeration of mountainous castles. As they passed the point of the butte, the valley opened wide, showing a good-sized lake, about a mile long and half-mile wide, that lay in the shadow of the butte.

They now followed the west edge of the valley, the trail riding between the shoulders of the mountains and the Yellowstone River. It was an uneventful and even monotonous ride, although Gabe and Ezra never tired of the mountain scenery and Wolf enjoyed his freedom to roam without the responsibility to scout ahead. Gabe grinned when the big black canine trotted back alongside, a tuft of rabbit fur dangling from his jowls. "You're just like Ezra, always hungry!" declared Gabe leaning down to speak to the Wolf.

"I heard that!" answered Ezra from behind him. "But I can't argue with it either!"

"Well, we'll prob'ly be stoppin' soon, so maybe you can get that woman of yours to feed you again!" said Gabe, twisting around in his seat to look at his friends. He saw Dove smiling but when Ezra turned to look at her, she looked away as if she hadn't heard. When he turned back to speak to Gabe, she called out, "He said he's wants fish! So, you two will have to catch some soon!"

"See there!" replied Ezra, "No sooner do you open your mouth," speaking to Gabe, "than she's got me working again!"

"Work? Since when do you call fishing work?" jibed Gabe.

"Well, it ain't the same as sleepin' in the shade!" answered Ezra, laughing.

Gabe shook his head, turned back to look to the trail and got his first glimpse of the Yellowstone Lake is the distance. The massive blue gem lay like a smooth table top, but he had assumed it to be even larger. What he did not know was he saw only the southeast arm of the lake and that it would take a full day's travel for them to go from their camp of this night to the northernmost edge of the lake.

Cougar Woman led them past the wide cut bank of the river to a grassy plain at the edge of a sandbar at water's edge. The site was in the shadow of a flat-topped mesa that held juniper on its shoulder and offered cover for their camp. Without a word, Cougar Woman and the two warriors stepped down and stripped the gear from their mounts, and Snake Eater led the three horses to water's edge. Gabe and company reined up together and swung down, with Dove going to the pannier for the cookware, but Ezra went to her side and spoke softly, "I don't know what's goin' on with those three, but you don't have to cook for them, just us, and I'll help you."

"I saw they were staying by themselves all day, is something wrong?" she asked.

"Dunno. Might be that Little Mountain is jealous of Gabe, or somethin' else, I can't figger it out, neither can Gabe."

Dove nodded, understanding, then added, "If Cougar Woman comes or speaks, then we can do different. If not, I will cook just for us."

Ezra nodded, took the lead for her buckskin, and finished stripping the horses to take them to water. Gabe had dropped his gear and the packs from the roan near the trees, then helped Ezra drop the travois. The two friends led the horses and the mule to the water and rubbed them down as they drank and snatched mouthfuls of grass at river's edge. Ezra looked back at the camp, saw the two warriors talking with Cougar Woman and spoke to Gabe, "I told Dove she didn't have to cook for them others, unless Cougar Woman spoke to her or decided to help."

Gabe looked at him with a bit of a frown, "Sounds reasonable. Not her job, I'm just happy she includes me in the meals."

Ezra scowled, "It took some convincin', had to threaten to spank her a mite, but she finally allowed it would be alright for you to be eatin' with us."

Gabe laughed, "If I had to guess, she prob'ly had to convince you to share with me! What with you wantin' to eat everything that even resembles food."

***

They picketed the horses on the grass and walked back to the campsite together. Ezra said he would help Dove by going for some trout while Gabe took his usual trek to the hilltop for his looksee. Gabe went to his packs, slipped the scope from the saddle bags and started up the hill. As he made a switchback turn to go to the crest, he looked back at the camp, hoping to see Cougar Woman coming from the trees, but there was nothing. Wolf had stopped when he paused to look around, but as he looked back to the crest, Wolf started off at a run to beat his friend to the top of the flat mesa. They went to the edge, sat down and started his survey of the valley beyond and the nearby hills and valleys.

He spotted three moose at the edge of a backwater pool, the bull walking into the chest deep water, sticking his head underwater and coming up with water lilies on his massive rack, and looking around as he munched on the fresh shoots from the water. A bunch of mule deer, seven in all, were making their way to the water's edge for their evening drink, and eight big horn sheep, three rams, the rest ewes and lambs were watching over the valley from a high up rocky hillside. But nothing else of any size moved anywhere. Gabe lowered the scope and leaned back on his elbows beside Wolf and enjoyed the panoramic vista. The sun was sitting on the western horizon, readying its palette of colors for its dusky display. Gabe looked at the clouds that hung in the blue sky, knowing the sun would soon paint their underbellies with a variety of colors from pink to gold and everything in between. He breathed deep of the mountain air, enjoying his moments of solitude, and thought of the times he and Pale Otter had enjoyed just watching the sunset and sunrise, the morning always her favorite. Then he thought of her and Cougar Woman, realizing for a short while he had considered Cougar Woman for, for what? A wife, a friend, a companion, or . . .? And he felt as if he was betraying the memory of Pale Otter. But he shook his head and thought, *Doesn't make any difference, she's made it pretty plain that she has no interest.* He looked at Wolf, ran his fingers through his friend's scruff and said, "C'mon boy, maybe we can help Ezra catch some trout for supper!"

He slipped the scope in its case, rose, and with a wave, sent Wolf on his way back to camp, or to go roaming for his supper or maybe to find himself a furry friend. Gabe smiled as he walked down the trail, random thoughts filling his mind, as he enjoyed the smell of pine and the clear mountain air.

A finger of aspen came from the draw behind the camp and stood at the edge of the trees that shadowed the camp site. The trail from the hilltop cut through the close growing aspen and into the assorted ponderosa and juniper. Gabe had stepped into the darker timber, when he was struck on the side of his head with a blow that sent him reeling and tumbling onto the long pine needles at the base of a ponderosa. He rolled as he hit the ground, looking back at whatever struck him and saw the big Shoshone, Little Mountain, rushing toward him. The big man lifted his foot as he growled, wanting to stomp the chest of Gabe, but Gabe saw his move and rolled away, coming to his feet, arms outstretched. "What're you doin'?" he asked, dropping into a crouch as the man came toward him.

"I will kill you!" snarled the man. He lowered his shoulders and charged toward Gabe with arms outstretched, wanting to grab the smaller man in a bear hug to crush him. Gabe stepped back and Little Mountain rushed, but Gabe grabbed at the man's arms and fell backwards, bringing his assailant with him, dropped to his back and with his feet at the man's midriff, catapulted him overhead.

Little Mountain crashed into the rough bark of a tall ponderosa and slid to the ground on his head and shoulders, but for a big man, he was exceptionally agile and was on his feet facing Gabe as soon as the smaller man turned. Again the big man charged, roaring as he came. Gabe feinted to the right, and stepped to his left, ducked under the massive arm, and buried his right fist in Little Mountain's gut, and brought his left fist down in a chop behind his ear, dropping him to the ground.

Gabe stepped back, watching the big man roll to the side, look at Gabe with wide eyes and come to his feet, a little slower than before. The two combatants, both in a crouch, circled one another, watching each other. Gabe made a feinting move to the right, but Little Mountain did not move, so Gabe landed a stiff jab to the man's nose, breaking it and splattering blood across his lower face, startling the man who was not used to anything resembling boxing in a fight. He brought up a hand to his face to feel his nose and Gabe brought a roundhouse right to his jaw, that staggered the big man who stumbled to his right into the branches of a juniper. He kicked back at the low tree limbs, and in a rage, charged at Gabe again.

Gabe danced side to side, but the man came on and as he neared, Gabe stepped to the left, under the man's big arm, and brought his arm across Little Mountain's chest whose momentum upended him and Gabe drove him into the ground, knocking the wind from his lungs and driving his head into the ground. The big man was dazed, slowly rolled to the side, and came to his hands and knees, shaking his head and looking back at Gabe. He rose to his knees, and started to get to his feet, but Gabe quickly stepped close and brought a chopping left to his head and another roundhouse right to his face, smashing his lips against his teeth and splattering blood. The man teetered, then Gabe stepped close, turned away and spun around and used his left leg in a swinging kick that almost took the man's head off, knocking him to his back, bending him backwards over his knees and rendering him unconscious.

Gabe put his hands on his knees, breathing heavy, and watching the big man's chest rise and fall in gasping breaths but he did not move. When Gabe caught his breath, he walked nearer the big man, saw he was still unconscious, then shook his head and walked back to camp. Ezra was walking up from the river's edge, two forked sticks with big trout hanging in his hands and a grin that rivaled the setting sun showing his pride in his work. Gabe smiled, walked to his friend and relieved him of one of the sticks, looked at the fish, "You did good! These are gonna be great!"

They walked to the fire where Dove and Cougar Woman waited. The women smiled at the sight of the fish, and Dove looked to Cougar Woman, "I told you my man would bring many!" Cougar Woman looked at Gabe, "Did you get those?"

"No, Ezra did all the fishin'. I was up yonder, takin' a looksee."

"Did you see anything?" asked Cougar Woman, somewhat guardedly.

"Oh, saw some moose, deer, bighorns, and some beautiful scenery."

"That's all? Nothing else?"

"Oh, I bumped into Little Mountain back in the trees yonder. I think he decided to take a nap in the shade. But that's all," answered Gabe. He saw the bit of a frown on Cougar Woman's face and was unsure whether she knew about Little Mountain's plans, but chose not to speak of it, leaving any explanation to her.

For the first time, Cougar Woman helped Dove with the preparations of the meal. The fish were seasoned, caked in river mud, and laid at the edge of the coals, then more coals pulled over the top of them. While they baked, Dove prepared some corn pone and Cougar Woman tended to some roasting Camas bulbs. Nearby sat a birchbark bowl with a variety of berries, choke cherries, service berries and raspberries. Gabe leaned back and Cougar Woman handed him a cup of hot coffee, smiling as she did, then turning back to her work. Gabe smiled, thinking, *Maybe I was wrong about her.*

"I like this coffee," declared Cougar Woman as she handed Gabe a cupful. She sat down near him, but the two warriors were opposite the fire and both scowled at the two. As Gabe lifted the cup to his lips, Snake Eater growled, "Our war leader is not to serve you!"

Gabe lowered the cup, looked at Cougar Woman and back at Snake Eater, "I have never known a warrior to try to tell the war leader what they were to do. What gives you the right to question your leader?" He did not raise his voice nor scowl at the man, but the even tone of his words reflected only a question.

Snake Eater looked from Gabe to Little Mountain and back to Gabe. He stood as if to try to intimidate, "Our leader does not serve, but is served!"

"Then why don't you serve her? She wanted coffee, you did not move, nor did Little Mountain. She does not need to serve nor to be served, she is a leader and does as she will, would you question her?" asked Gabe.

Snake Eater stared at Gabe, glanced at Cougar Woman, and slowly seated himself, grumbling under his breath.

Cougar Woman looked at the two warriors, "I chose you because you are brave warriors. You are needed if we were to fight others, like the Blackfoot. I did not need you to protect me or try to tell me what to do. This man has fought beside us and for us, while you hid behind a rock, he took the fight to the Blackfoot and sent them away bloodied." She paused, breathed deep, nodded toward Little Mountain, "And he has shown himself strong in face to face fighting, has he not, Little Mountain?"

The big warrior sat sullen, staring at the smoldering coals, his eyes almost swollen shut, his nose flattened and askew, his lip swollen. He winced as he moved, grunted an answer to his leader and tried to chew on a piece of smoked meat.

"If I choose to be with this man, that is not your concern. If you no longer wish to scout with me, then go!" she pointed back to the trail they traveled the day before, "It has always been the way of our people that no one can make another do what he does not wish to do. When I chose you to join this scout, you made the choice to come. If you cannot do as you should, then leave!" Her words were concise and firm, her expression dour, and her resolve evident. Her nostrils flared as she sat, one leg outstretched before her, the other bent back at her side, a position she could quickly rise from if necessary. Gabe noticed she also had a hand on the haft of her knife as if she was ready to scalp the men before her and Gabe thought she could and would easily do that.

Snake Eater leaned back, slowly lowering his eyes and breathing deeply, then glanced at Little Mountain who still stared at the coals, and said, "We will stay."

"Then we will hear no more of this!" demanded Cougar Woman.

***

As they prepared to leave camp, Cougar Woman, within earshot of her warriors, directed Gabe, "You and Wolf take the point. We will cross the river there," pointing to a wide shallow downstream from their camp where the river bent back on itself, "and take the trail below the bluffs. It will follow the shore until a butte forces it behind."

Gabe nodded, whistled Wolf close, mounted up and led out. He smiled to himself, knowing Cougar Woman was showing her warriors that she was the leader, even over those from the other village. But it mattered little to Gabe, he preferred to be on point anyway, even though he still led the roan packhorse. The time alone with his thoughts was time treasured by Gabe, having come to appreciate the solitude.

Ebony readily stepped into the water, cold and fast moving though it was, the gravel bottom offered good footing and the water was no deeper than the knees on the long-legged stallion. They crossed one sandbar, then another and soon rose up the far bank where Wolf was shaking and rolling, trying to free himself of the cold water. Ebony joined in the action, as did the roan, both rolling their hides and shaking off the excess that had splashed on their bellies after they stepped off the last sandbar. But both animals eagerly stretched out, taking to the oft-used game trail that followed the shore of the Yellowstone Lake.

Once across the river, the trail took to the shoulder of a high rising hill that showed its granite face to the valley. The lower slopes showed an abundance of downed grey tree trunks, apparently victims of a winter storm blow-down, and the littered hillside was sprouting new growth trees, juniper, cedar and ponderosa. After passing the granite faced point, the trail moved away from the river that now sloshed through boggy ground, that bore cat-tail swamps, willow groves, and grassy topped bogs. As the trail rose above the valley floor, they could see the many different river beds that carried the Yellowstone River in high water and low, carving its snake like signature across the valley bottom.

They crossed the valley of another creek and moved through a patch of timber, thick with fir and spruce that stood tall, catching the wind in the high branches and letting it whistle on its way past. Then they crossed the bald face of a spur that fell from a limestone ridge that marked the tip of a long line of mountains that stretched back to the east, rising higher and higher. A wide hollow at the base of another spur beckoned the travelers to take a mid-day breather. They were on a timbered point that pushed into the southeast arm of the big lake, offering a view of the bigger body of water to the northwest. While the horses grazed and the others lounged in the shade, Gabe and Ezra walked the narrow sandy beach, looking at the dark blue of the deep waters. Gabe bent down and picked up a flat stone, side armed it to the water and watched it skip across the smooth mountain mirror. Ezra did the same, both men laughing as they competed for who could skip the most, but soon tired and continued their walk.

"So, you gettin' interested in Cougar Woman?" asked Ezra, trying to be nonchalant in his questioning.

Gabe stopped, turned to look at his friend, "Why would any man be interested in a woman that could probably lick him in a fight?"

Ezra laughed, "You might be right about that. But, are you?"

Gabe walked on, thinking, picked up and skipped another stone, "I dunno," he answered. "She's quite a woman," he added.

Ezra said, "Dove thinks the two of you would make a good pair."

"Oh, she does, does she? That don't mean much. It seems every woman that sees an unattached man thinks the next woman is the right match, anything to get him hitched!"

Ezra scowled, "You know, that does seem to be the way of 'em, don't it?" he paused, then stopped and turned to face his friend, "So, what happened with you and Little Mountain?"

Gabe drawled, "Like I told Cougar Woman, I just bumped into him on the way back to camp."

Ezra shook his head, knowing that was all he would get out of his friend, but the damage done to Little Mountain's face told enough of the story. They turned back and strolled along the beach, returning to the temporary camp just as Dove and Cougar Woman rose from their grassy seats in the shade of a tall spruce.

***

The afternoon trek followed the trail through thick black timber, crossing two more creeks and a wide meadow before ducking back into the dark timber. When the trail rose to top a long bald limestone butte, Gabe left the trail to go to the knob at the end of the long butte. He stepped down and standing beside

Ebony's head, the rein hanging loosely in his hand, he took in the magnificent panorama. Before him lay the vast Yellowstone lake, the darker blues showing the great depths, the varying shades of azure and cobalt revealing the different flows and underwater features. The wind was picking up and Gabe leaned into it, watching the water move, making whitecaps that chased one another toward the shore below. To his left he saw the long peninsula that separated the south and southeast arms of the lake, and directly across the water, about three miles, lay a solitary island where, Gabe surmised, no man had ever trod. To his right, the water stretched another fifteen to twenty miles, but the wind carried mist hampered his view. He wiped his face, turned back to the Black who stood, head down, waiting, swung aboard and turned back to take shelter in the tall timber.

When he dropped off the knob, the trail soon broke into the open where another creek carved its way to the lake. On the far side of the creek and upstream from where he stood, lay a wide grassy meadow, suitable for the horses. He stepped down and stripped his horse and the pack horse, dropping the gear at the foot of a big spruce, and rubbed the horses down. He picketed them on the grass and began gathering firewood for their camp. He no sooner returned to his chosen site, than the others rode from the trees, and joined him in his preparations.

***

The second day on the lake trail was little different than the first, until late morning when they broke from the timber to round a point and move across the flats that held two patches of white and pink sand and clay that stood in sharp contrast to the deep green of the pines. They rounded the northeast end of the lake, staying with the trail that turned to the west, until Cougar Woman took the lead to take them across a boggy bottom stretch that held a twisting shallow creek that danced back and forth through the willows and cattails. A slash of white gypsum scarred the far riverbank, with a greater deposit of either gypsum or calcite cutting a slash across the face of a low hill to the northwest.

Cougar Woman took them on a trail that cut through the timber below the white slash and led them to the bank of the Yellowstone river as it carried fresh water from the lake toward the flats below. Cougar Woman chose a familiar campsite, obviously used before and recently, at the edge of the trees that overlooked the river and the promised encampment site beyond. She twisted around to look at Gabe, pointed to the valley beyond, "That is where the encampment will be, but we will camp here tonight."

"From the looks of that smoke, there's already some folks there," answered Gabe, nodding toward the flats beyond the timber covered ridge and the spirals of cook fire smoke.

"That would be the *Agaideka,* they have been here preparing for the others. We will join them tomorrow when we have time to prepare our camp as well."

Gabe slowly lifted his head in a nod, understanding, but also anxious to make camp one last time before meeting up with so many others. He never did like crowds, anyway.

11 / ENCAMPMENT

Gabe stood in his stirrups, eyes wide, shading his eyes with his hand as the rising sun stretched his shadow across the slope before him. He looked across the water of the Yellowstone River to see white clouds rising from behind the trees and dissipating just above tree tops. He turned to see a wide grinning Cougar Woman watching him. "What is that!?" he asked, pointing behind him.

He twisted back around as she came up beside him, "That is the beginning of the land of many smokes," she answered.

"But that smell! It's like rotten eggs or somethin'! Whew!" he lifted his neckerchief up to cover his nose, his forehead creased as he made his face at the disgusting odor that came from the direction of the steam plumes.

"The pools and pond, the springs, and mud. They boil and stink." She nodded toward a whitish grey pool below them, the ground about it the same color as the liquid that gurgled within. Dead trees lay rotting on the slight slope above and the flat beyond the stink water pool. The runoff from the pool led to the water of the Yellowstone, spreading on the low sandbar and showing green as it colored the water of the river. But the worst of the stench and the steam plumes rose on the far shores of the river and back into the trees.

The mud pots and cauldrons bubbled and spewed, the hot springs and geysers fumed and spat, and Gabe and company sat and stared. Steam clouds lifted and danced above the hot waters and the wind carried varying wafts of pungent sulfurous smells their way. Ezra lifted his neckerchief over his nose as he muttered, "My pa used to preach about Hell and the smell of Sulphur and the heat. Have we come upon Hell an' nobody told me?"

Gabe shook his head, looked at Cougar Woman, "Is there a lot of this?"

"Yes, but not close. And there are other places like this. There are some that shoot water higher than the tallest trees!"

Gabe frowned, glanced at Ezra and back at Cougar Woman, but found himself speechless. He didn't want to question her truthfulness, but he would have to chew on that awhile before he swallowed that as the full truth. He saw Ezra's eyebrows lift at his unspoken question, but when his shoulders lifted in a deep sigh, he knew he was thinking much the same. He turned his attention back to the spectacle, saw more steam clouds rising, some little geysers trying to erupt, and another strong waft of the stench, and he turned away, to follow Cougar Woman off the ridge.

"I see Little Mountain and Snake Eater are not with us, did they decide to leave?" asked Gabe as he rocked back and forth in the saddle, Ebony cautiously stepping down the steep slope. Cougar Woman spoke over her shoulder, "I sent them on to the camp. It is just around that bend," she nodded to the north where the river made a bend to the west. "We will cross there," she pointed to the crook of the bend where a long crescent shaped sandbar divided the waters of the river, making both branches spread across a gravelly bottom and offered a good crossing.

They crossed the river, rode the shoulder of a wide basin, and mounted a low rising ridge. As they crested the low ridge, Cougar Woman reined up and waited for the others. When Gabe rode up beside her on the left, she looked back to see Ezra and Dove coming alongside on her right. A broad park stretched out before them, rolling land that sported grass aplenty, a stream on the east and another on the west edge, islands of thick timber interspersed in the broad plain, and a white scar showing a sulfur spring that lay nearer the river.

Near a wide patch of timber, and next to the west edge of the park, several tipis lifted their poles and thin spirals of smoke. Cougar Woman said, "That is the camp of the *Agaideka.*" She looked to Dove, "Do your people camp near them, or others?" referring to those already camped.

"We will camp there," pointing to the area at the far end of the park, a stretch of grassy land that lay between the two creeks.

"Then my people will be there," stated Cougar Woman, pointing to an area adjacent to the one chosen by Dove, yet close to the west creek. "Both streams have good water, and our camps will be upstream from the others. There are trees there for cover if needed and we will be close," added Cougar Woman, looking at Gabe when she mentioned being close. She pointed into the distance, "And beyond that creek is where the combined horse herd will be kept."

Gabe stared into the distance, saw the rolling hills that showed green with an abundance of grass, and knew the people usually kept the herd close, but together, although some warriors preferred having their war ponies or buffalo hunting ponies near their lodge, choosing to take them to pasture and water individually. Gabe thought he would probably do that with Ebony, preferring the stallion to be by himself and not get into a fight with another over the herd mares. Beyond the rolling grassy hills rose some black timbered foothills that would be a natural barrier for the herd, and they would stay near their graze and water.

"Well, let's go get this lodge set up," suggested Ezra. "I'm anxious to stop an' relax a spell."

"Sound's good to me," answered Gabe, gigging Ebony to a trot, pulling the lead line to the pack horse taut jerking his arm back behind him, as he started to the chosen site. The others followed, at a walk, laughing at Gabe's antics as he dragged the roan, neck stretched out, behind him.

They chose a site close to the tree line, knowing the rest of the camp would lay between them and the bulk of the encampment and if there was any solitude to be found, it would be in the trees. The tipi went up quickly, the men doing the work under the guidance of Dove, and as soon as it was finished, she instructed them to haul in the gear as she arranged the inside to suit her plans. Wolf found some shade out of the way and snoozed while the others worked. Cougar had gone in search of Little Mountain and Snake Eater for them to make their camp nearby and in the trees behind the chosen site for their people, the *Tukkutikka*.

***

During the next three days, groups, from families to villages, filtered into the encampment grounds and took their places, setting up their hide lodges or building brush huts or other shelters. Each village separated from the others by border space and room for leading horses to the pasture. Arbors were built for some of the ceremonies, a central compound was arranged in the middle of the broad park with many of the leaders' lodges forming the circle. There was an arbor nearby where the leaders would meet for their conferences, planning the fall buffalo hunt, the next encampment, and tending to matters that involved the entire tribe. Both the village of Dove and the village of Cougar Woman had arrived and set up their lodges, arranging the village as was the custom with the shaman and war leader's lodges centered within the setting and facing the central compound. As expected, Dove's lodge was at the westernmost perimeter at the tree line and somewhat isolated from the others, which was as Gabe and Ezra planned.

"There will be several dances, and I have heard talk of a new ceremony called the sun dance, but I know little about it," said Cougar Woman as she sat near the fire circle in front of Dove's hide lodge.

"I have heard of this also, it has to do with young warriors earning honors, from what I am told," replied Dove. Neither Ezra nor Gabe were privy to the conversations of the warrior societies where topics like this were discussed, but it did not concern them anyway. They were seated near the lodge, using woven willow backrests that had been made by the sisters their first year as wives.

"We're gettin' low on coffee, thought I'd take a ride

in the area, see if I could find some chicory," drawled Ezra, sipping at the hot brew in the cup before him.

"You mean all that I brought from St. Louis is gone already?" asked an incredulous Gabe, picking up a small twig and tossing it to the fire ring, that held nothing but greyed coals.

"No, it's not gone, just thought it'd last longer if I had some roasted chicory to add to it, like we done before."

The quiet moment dragged on as the men lazed in the morning sun, watching the activity of the encampment below them. They had chosen the highest point of the park, on the west edge where the terrain sloped away from the mountains behind, and their view encompassed the entire park, the river at the northernmost edge and the hills beyond. The park had sprouted many more lodges and now showed the hawk's nest formation of tipi poles from around a hundred lodges, and Cougar Woman had said there were still more that would arrive within the next couple days.

Gabe nodded toward the cluster of lodges, "That there looks a lot like many of the cities back east. What'chu figger, three, four hundred people?"

"At least. Mebbe more. But it'll only be for a week or so, shouldn't be too hard to handle. Most o' these folks are mighty clean 'bout their mornin' business, an' such. Better'n most towns of the civilized folks," observed Ezra.

"That St. Louis now, that place stunk all the time. The gutters of the streets were runnin' sewers, couldn't hardly walk without smellin' that stuff. Then the smoke from the stoves an' the smells from the tanneries, whooeee! I was almighty thankful I had a place to stay outta town an' away from there. Somebody said there was more'n two thousand people there an' more comin' in ever' day." Gabe shook his head at the remembrance, "Made me homesick for the mountains more'n I ever thought possible."

Ezra shook his head as he pictured such a sight, emitted a heavy sigh that lifted his shoulders, and changed directions with their talk, "Have you noticed we ain't seen Little Mountain and Snake Eater since we got camp set up? Wonder what they been up to?"

The women looked their way when they heard the mention of the two warriors and Cougar Woman answered, "They have been talking to the council. Little Mountain wants to challenge me as war leader."

Gabe looked at her, frowning, "Is it because of us?"

Cougar Woman dropped her eyes, "He does not like that we are friends. But he has wanted to be war leader since before I was chosen. He also wanted me for his woman, but I would not have him. If I were not war leader, my father could choose a man for me, set a bride price and make me become the woman of whoever he chose. But as a war leader, I can choose my own mate."

"This challenge, what happens?" asked Gabe.

"We fight," she answered, simply.

Gabe frowned and asked, "You will have to fight him? He's twice as big as you!" Then he had a thought, "Can you choose someone to fight in your place?" hopeful of the chance.

Cougar woman let a grin split her face, then shook her head, "No, if I am to be the war leader, I must fight my own battles. No one would follow me if I cannot fight anyone that challenges."

"And when will this happen?"

"Whenever the council agrees," answered a somber Cougar Woman.

"If you lose, what then?" asked Gabe.

"If I live, then I will just be a warrior of my people as I was before I was chosen."

"What about your father choosing a mate?" queried Gabe, concerned.

"He has that right, but my father respects me and I do not believe he would make me become the mate of a man if I did not want that man."

Gabe breathed deep, exhaled loudly as he stifled his frustration at the way of the people, then asked, "If you fight, may we be there?" motioning to Ezra, Dove and himself.

"Yes."

Gabe lowered his head and mumbled, "If he hurts you, I might have to finish what we started in the woods!"

12 / STOLEN

Gabe and Ezra sat opposite one another, using a large flat rock as a table top while they cleaned their weapons. Both were working on pistols, having cleaned the rifles first, as usual, when Cougar Woman rode up to their camp, obviously in a hurry and concerned. Gabe stood as she approached, "What is it? What's wrong?" he asked.

"A band of the *Agaideka* were attacked on their way to the encampment. They were few and the Hidatsa killed most of the men and took captives," explained Cougar Woman, looking from Gabe to Ezra, her erratic movements showing her frustration and anger.

"So, what does that mean?" asked Gabe, judging by her actions he was thinking that she was going after the raiders. "If there's to be war party that goes after them, isn't that up to the chief of the *Agaideka?*"

"Yes, but many of their warriors are a part of the Sun Dance and have been in isolation and prayer. For

them to leave would break the spell of the Sun Dance
and their prayers to the Sun God."

Gabe frowned, "So, they're not going to go after
the Hidatsa?"

"*Owitze,* Twisted Hand, the chief, asked for others
to join their war leader, Shoots Running Buffalo, to go
after the Hidatsa. The war leader said he knows you,
and asked if you would come," said Cougar Woman,
frowning slightly with her head cocked to the side,
wondering about this man that was known by others
of her people.

Gabe looked to Ezra, "What'chu think?" He glanced
to Dove, who was preparing some camas roots for their
meal, saw her looking at her husband, and added, "Maybe
you should stay with your woman and little one."

Ezra finished wiping down the pistol, started loading it and looked at Gabe, "Oh, I think she'll be safe
enough here with all these," nodding to the encampment. Then he looked at his wife, "What about you,
Dove. Think I should go?"

"If it was our child, I would want you to go," she
replied simply.

Ezra looked at Gabe, nodded, and finished loading
the pistol. Gabe turned to Cougar Woman, "How soon?"

"We will gather at the lodge of the war leader, there,"
she pointed to the cluster of tipis of the *Agaideka,* that
lay near the Yellowstone River on the north edge of
the encampment. "I will return as soon as I collect my

weapons and food." Without awaiting an answer, she swung aboard her mount and headed to her camp.

Gabe marveled at the woman every time he saw her riding the strawberry roan gelding. The two were extensions of each other, and she rode with nothing more than a blanket held in place with a woven girth and rawhide stirrups, but he had often seen her command the horse with nothing more than a shift of her weight, leg pressure, or even a spoken word. He watched her ride away, then turned to the lodge to secure his gear.

**

"Spirit Bear, Black Buffalo, it is good to have you with us," declared Shoots Running Buffalo, the war leader for the village of the *Agaideka.* He nudged his mount closer to the big black of Gabe, "The Hidatsa that hit our people killed four warriors, their women and sons. They took five young women captive. The rest, three warriors, two old women, three little ones, came in when the sun was high to tell of the attack. They said they saw two hands and two warriors."

Cougar Woman was on the far side of Gabe but heard the report, and asked, "How far?"

"Below the canyon of the yellow stone."

Cougar Woman nodded, knowing the place, and looked at Gabe to explain, "From here, most of a day, that will put them two days ahead."

Gabe shook his head, quickly calculating, thinking *this will take all of a week, maybe more.* He looked to Shoots Running Buffalo, "Did your men do any damage?"

"He said there were three Hidatsa killed, maybe two wounded."

"Maybe that'll slow 'em down a mite, but still . . ." began Gabe, but yielded to Shoots as he looked to the others. With Gabe, Ezra and Cougar Woman, there were six other warriors, making ten warriors going after a party of twelve that had already proven their willingness and ability to kill without hesitation, and might already have killed their captives. But if not, the captives would also slow them, and the size of the party would make tracking easy, allowing them to make good time in their pursuit.

Shoots had motioned to the others, and they started out at a canter, determined to make time while they could. Soon the terrain would be more challenging and the trails minimal, but they were familiar with the country, giving them a slight advantage. Shoots had taken the lead, with two of his chosen men directly behind him. Cougar was astride her strawberry roan and led Gabe, with Wolf at his side, and Ezra, while the remainder brought up the rear. The trail was wide and well-traveled by the many northern Shoshone making the trek to the encampment, and Shoots kept a good pace, varying the gait from a canter to a walk and more.

The gibbous moon was rising in the east as the

sun was cradled on the western mountains when they came to the scene of the attack. The bodies had been removed or buried, but the carcasses of two horses had drawn the carrion eaters. When the group came into the clearing, the flock of turkey buzzards flew up, wings beating the air with the muffled flutter, coyotes tucked tail and scampered away, ravens flew into the branches of a dead snag and raised their complaints, but a big badger refused to move as he burrowed into the chest cavity to retrieve his chosen morsels.

The group had slowed to a walk, showing respect for the lives lost at this site, but Shoots soon slapped his legs to his mount to pick up the pace and put the scene behind them. For another hour he pushed on, but as the curtain of dusk was dropping, he reined up at a small clearing above the crumbled bank of the river and stepped down. They led their horses to water, stripped the gear and rubbed them down before picketing them on the graze.

As they gathered near the small fire that one of the men had kindled, Gabe asked, "Are we gonna push on by the moon?" he asked, looking up at the off-kilter orb that seemed to be looking down on them. It was a clear night and the stars were beginning to show their faces, the darkness bringing the coolness, but the moon offered its blue tinted glow to guide them.

"We will rest the horses, start again soon," answered Shoots.

Cougar was beside Gabe and asked, "Were any of the captives a part of your family?" She had noticed their leader seemed a little angrier than what would be usual, and he had shown more determination.

"One of the captives is the daughter of my brother. He was killed there," nodding back on the trail toward the battle site. "She is a girl of twelve winters, Sacajawea. I gave her that name. She liked going with me in the canoe, and I saw her as a warrior such as you," he nodded toward Cougar as he spoke.

"Have you fought the Hidatsa before?" asked Gabe, chewing on his Depuyer as he leaned against the grey log.

"Yes, the Hidatsa, some call them Minnetaree, they are with other Sioux bands, and have attacked our people before, always to get women for their men. Their women are fat and ugly, but not ours. They are allies with the Crow, sometimes. They also take women to trade to the French for rifles. They have strange headdresses, and they mark themselves, like this," pointing to a tattooed band around his bicep, "only much more. And they are fierce fighters," explained Shoots Running Buffalo.

"So, they will not kill the captives?" asked Ezra.

"No, but if the captive is trouble, they will kill."

***

They rested for a little more than two hours, and when the moon was high and the night was still, they started again. They moved west across the foothills, leaving the trail followed by the Hidatsa that shadowed the Yellowstone River. By first light, they dropped from the hills into the wide valley carved by the river and discovered the camp of the raiders near the river. After a quick examination of the sign, Shoots looked up, "They spent the night, left at first light." He looked down the trail, shook his head, and Gabe knew what the man was feeling and thinking, wanting to push on, overtake them and recover the captives. But the Hidatsa were on fresh horses, and theirs were tired. He motioned to the others to get down, "We will eat and rest the horses. We could overtake them before nightfall."

They stripped the horses, rubbed them down and put them on the graze. Gabe had packed light and did not bring a coffee pot nor coffee, and the men sat stoic, thinking how good it would taste about now. Cougar Woman sat nearby, watching the two friends, and asked, "Why do you do this?"

Gabe frowned, "Do what?"

"You are not Shoshone, you do not need to be here, but you are, why?"

Gabe looked at Ezra, back to Cougar, "Well, we're as close to the Shoshone as we are to our own family. We have lived with the Shoshone, married into the tribe, and it's the right thing to do. As Dove said, 'if it were her child, she would want us to go.'"

"Ummhmm," added Ezra, "and when Dove was taken by the Blackfoot, Shoots Running Buffalo was right beside me when we caught up with them and rescued Dove, so . . ." he shrugged.

Cougar Woman lifted her head, looking at the two, understanding, but still finding it difficult to believe for what they were doing was contrary to what she had been taught about the other people, those that were crowding in on the land of her people.

Their conversation was interrupted when Shoots came near, another man with him, and stood before them. "When we fought together before, you had gone ahead and stopped the band of the Blackfoot until we could come from behind. Would you want to do that again?"

Gabe let a slow grin tug at the corner of his mouth as he looked up at Shoots, "I reckon I could do that. Is that what this fella is here for?" nodding to the warrior beside Shoots.

"This is Black Dog; he will guide you." He stepped back, pointed to valley of the Yellowstone and the hills that rose on the north, "There is a trail there, it will take you over those hills and to the river. If you make good time, you will be there before the Hidatsa. It is up to you what you do then. You will be there by nightfall. We will wait, but we will be ready by first light."

Gabe looked at Ezra, "You wanna come with me, or stay with them?"

Ezra chuckled, "We ain't been in a good fight together in some time. I'll go with you."

Cougar Woman looked at Shoots Running Buffalo, "Where will I be best used?"

He looked from Gabe to Ezra, back to Cougar, "You choose."

She nodded, looked at Gabe and said, "I would learn of your ways."

He smiled, looked at Shoots, "We'll give the horses time to rest, then we'll be on our way."

13 / RECONNOITER

Their trail rose above the river, riding the shoulders of the northern mountains, across the face of a high basin and over the saddle of the mountainous ridge. It was a long climb and rough country, but once over the saddle they dropped into another basin. "Let's give the horses a breather," suggested Gabe, reining Ebony to the edge of the trees. They were below the crest of a dome like mountain, and the east face was covered with black timber, but they were beside a thicket of aspen and a small spring fed pool offered fresh water for the animals.

As they found a seat on the grassy slope below the aspen, each one stretched out, letting the horses enjoy the grasses below the spring. Gabe looked at Black Dog, "It looked like the river went into a bit of a canyon on the other side of this dome, is that right?"

"Yes, but there are different camps there. Shoots Buffalo thinks they will camp there this night," answered Black Dog.

Gabe looked to Cougar Woman, "Do you know that canyon?"

"Yes, I have been there. The trail is on the far side and there are two other creeks, one narrow, the other at the end. The canyon is short, but there are good camps. The near side is too steep for an attack, the far side too rocky, rough. But the other end, and the valley, both have good places for an ambush." She sat with knees drawn up, arms locked before them, legs crossed at her ankles, as she looked at Gabe and Ezra.

Wolf lay at Gabe's side, disinterested and unmoving. Gabe idly ran his fingers through the thick scruff, thinking, then looked down the long draw that followed the contours of the mountain and rode the tree line. In the distance, about three miles below, he saw the thin ribbon of the Yellowstone winding its way lazily through the valley, sheltered on both banks by a band of greenery, while the remainder of the valley and slopes from the western mountains showed shades of grey and brown dimpled with the blue greens of sage and rabbit brush.

It was mid-afternoon and the horses needed rest, but the trail before them was downhill and easygoing, and Gabe was anxious to get a close-up look at the ambush sites Cougar spoke about, and to find the whereabouts of the raiders. He stood and stretched, picked up a stick and swatted at the kinnikinnick bush beside them, knocking some of the partially ripe green and red berries onto the ground.

He was frustrated, uncertain about what to do next. He walked aimlessly along the edge of the aspen, the leaves rattling and fluttering overhead. He had been in tighter straits than this before, the odds were not overwhelming and he and Ezra had tackled more than a dozen warriors before, even on this journey when the Blackfoot hunting party had attacked. But this bunch had captives that would be endangered by any attack and that concerned him. He knew little about the Hidatsa and what they might do to the captives if ambushed. He knew he, Ezra, and Cougar woman could probably take the warriors down, but what about the captives? Maybe instead of a head-on attack, if they could free the captives, or at least whittle the numbers down before an ambush, that might improve the chances of the captives going unharmed. But how?

He turned and started back to the group, searching the area for any movement or any indication of life, but nothing stirred except a fat yellow bellied marmot that sat atop a boulder, watching them and chewing something. *Oh, to have no more concern than where the next meal was coming from, that would be nice,* thought Gabe, shaking his head slightly. As he neared the others, he spoke up, "I'm gonna head on down, find a place where I can take a look-see and get a better idea of what we're facing."

"Ya need comp'ny?" asked Ezra.

"Nah. You let the horses rest. If I see anything or need ya, I'll let'chu know," answered Gabe, moving to Ebony's side. He tightened the girth, draped the reins over the black's neck and stepped into the stirrup and swung aboard. He nodded down the draw, "There 'pears to be a knob on the end of that ridge there. I'll prob'ly go up on it, but if that don't do, I'll find 'nother'n." He shook his head as he realized how his language had lapsed into the vernacular of the mountains. For all his life his father had chastised him whenever he failed to use proper grammar and respectful language, even after he attended university. If only he could hear him now.

From the crest of the knob he soon realized his view was obstructed with the shoulder of the dome mountain projecting into the valley and hiding the mouth of the canyon. He slipped the scope back in its case, snapped his finger to Wolf and returned to Ebony. They rounded the knob, turned back into a timbered draw and worked their way back toward the crest of the dome, then taking the shoulder to the bowl that lay below the edge. He tethered Ebony, and with rifle and scope in hand, he and Wolf walked to the bald crest of the shoulder and over the round top to drop to a secondary shoulder that overlooked the canyon below.

The river ran east to west in the canyon bottom, then at the mouth of the canyon made a wide bend to point to the north. The sun was rapidly lowering off his right shoulder, stretching the shadows along the canyon slopes into specter like phantoms that crawled across the rocky faces of the mountains. Even from this height, Gabe could hear the chuckling of the white water crashing over the rocks where the canyon pushed the river through narrows. As he lay on his belly, Wolf at his side, he scanned the canyon bottom, seeing the narrow shoulder on the south side, and the steep walls on the north. Then movement caught his eye and he focused on the south bank near the opening of the canyon. A line of riders stretched into the canyon, some side by side, others strung out in a line, and they rode to the wide shoulder at the base of a draw that carried a small stream from the mountains to cascade into the river below. This was the camp site Cougar had mentioned and the band was stopping and making camp.

With his scope stretched to its limit, he held it steady with his elbows resting on the ground before him, he tried to make out the captives and warriors. But the best he could do was count the horses, knowing each one held one rider. As they came together, and began sliding off their mounts, he counted. His first tally was thirteen. He stopped and thought, remembering Shoots Buffalo saying there were twelve warriors and five captives, so there should be seventeen. He scanned the group again, but with them dismounted, he could only count the horses, and again he counted thirteen. He shook his head, searched the group trying to make out the warriors and the captives by their actions, but the best he could make out was ten warriors and three captives, but even then he could not be sure. If that was an accurate count, that would mean they killed two captives, and lost two warriors. Shoots said the survivors told him that two warriors appeared to be wounded, so, maybe. *But, what about the captives?*

He moved the scope away from the band and searched the terrain around their camp, cataloging every rock, ridge, and gulley in his mind. The trees lay at the mountain's edge, the slope of the draw was steep, holding a narrow waterfall that split the camp, and the shoulder dropped to a steep bank into the river. But along the water's edge, there appeared to be a trail or at least a rocky shore. Another thorough scan, a look at the band, and Gabe slipped the scope back in its case and crabbed back away from the edge and turned in a crouch for the two of them to return to Ebony.

The others were waiting at the bottom of the timbered draw taken by Gabe to go to his shoulder look out, having followed his tracks around the first knob and choosing to wait at the bottom of the draw rather than climb another hillside. "I spotted 'em. They're makin' camp in the canyon by that first little creek." He spoke as he came from the trees, stopped momentarily as they remounted, "We can make camp at the bottom of this mountain where it flattens out at the tree line. We'll be well back and in the cover of the trees."

Black Dog asked, "Did you choose a place for ambush?"

They were strung out in single file, Black Dog behind Gabe, and Gabe twisted around in his saddle, giving Ebony his head to pick his way down the slope, "Not sure. We'll talk about it when we camp." Black Dog nodded and followed close behind. They had only traveled a mile when Gabe took to a slight shoulder covered with juniper and scattered ponderosa, reined up and stepped down, motioning to the others to make camp. From the edge of the camp, they could see the mouth of the canyon, but the sun was dropping below the western horizon and barely peeking over the mountains, making the distant hills appear as dark shadows as the golden lances stretched across the sky.

They had a cold camp, well protected in the trees and they drew close together to hear Gabe's idea. They had taken the horses to the river for their last drink of the night and picketed them in the trees. He used a stick to draw in the dirt, using the glow of the sunset to show his thoughts. "Here's the camp. It's about a hundred yards back from the river bank, in the shadow of the trees that hug the mountain, here. The trail stays on the shoulder along the south wall, nice and flat, but little cover. But, this bank," pointing to the edge of the squiggly line that represented the river, "on the south edge of the river, is about fifty feet above the water and it looks like there's a trail, or at least rocks, that could be followed all the way." He continued to explain the rest of his plan, detailing what each would do and where they would be as he spoke. "Also, I counted 'em. Shoots Buffalo said there were twelve warriors and five captives. But there's only thirteen people there. From what I could tell, there was only three captives." He lifted his eyes to each one as he spoke, waiting for their comments.

Cougar lifted her eyes from his dirt map, eyes flaring, "But, that means they have killed two of the captives!" she declared.

"Maybe. They were too far away to be sure. But that's the best I could tell. That also means that the two warriors that were wounded, didn't make it, which is a good thing," replied Gabe.

"But that would also mean they could easily kill the others," suggested Ezra.

The four were silent as they considered what they all thought, until Gabe said, "If they killed them, they did it even when they were not under attack, so that would mean the captives are in danger whether or not we attack."

The others looked at him, down at his dirt map, and back up, each one slowly nodding in agreement. And the prospects of a night attack made things even more risky, but they would have time to think about it and add to or change the plan if necessary. If they were to attack, it would be in the middle of the night, after most were tired and asleep and when the moon would be at its highest to give as much light as possible.

14 / AMBUSH

"You should not have killed her!" barked Big Horn. "She would have brought a big price from the French traders!" He glared at Spotted Elk, then dropped his eyes to the crumpled form of the girl. Blood covered her front, her head lay askew and the black hair tangled with thorns from the wait a bit brush when she tried to escape, spread across the pool of blood that pumped from the wide slit across her throat.

"She was running!" argued Spotted Elk. "That will keep the others from trying to escape! We are Hidatsa! No one escapes from the people!" He spun on his heel and went to the horses. Black Cloud was a fierce warrior, his stern image of broad sloping shoulders, the thin scalp lock that stood above his forehead, wrapped in red twine, and the many feathers that fluttered from the topknot of twisted hair at the back of his head, made a fearsome image. His fringed tunic with broad bands of beads over each shoulder was given him by the chief after he led a successful war party against the Arikara. His ever-present lance held scalp locks of the many defeated warriors of the Assiniboine, Arikara, and Crow. Grabbing a handful of mane, he swung up on his mount and viciously dug his heels into the horse's ribs, making the big red horse lunge forward and away from the pack. Big Horn mounted up and nodded to the others to come along. Ten warriors, including their war leader, *Cheshakhadakhi,* Lean Wolf, and four captives followed, spaced out with a warrior in front of and one behind each captive. The girls' hands were bound together with rawhide strips and the manes of the horses they rode were twisted in with the bindings. Their heads hung and one was seen sobbing as she twisted to look at the bloody form left beside the brush.

Big Horn, a warrior with many honors and also wearing several feathers from a top knot of hair, nudged his horse beside Spotted Elk, rode silently for a short way then asked, "You still want the one with long braids?"

Spotted Elk glared at his friend, grunted and replied, "I will take her to the Frenchman. He will pay for her. His woman needs another to keep him happy."

"You speak of Charbonneau?"

"Yes. He said if I bring him a good one to help Otter Woman, he will trade two rifles and powder and lead for her! Otter Woman is also Shoshone," he explained.

"But the others, they will want a share of the trade."

"Bah! They can have the other captives and share what they want. *Cheshakhadakhi,* has already claimed the fat one!" snarled Spotted Elk.

"They will fight for the others!" pleaded Big Horn.

"We will be gone," suggested Spotted Elk, leaning toward Big Horn. "We will leave the others and take the girl with us. We will get back to our village before they do and make the trade. They cannot do anything if it is done!" He had lowered his voice, glanced back at the others who trailed about twenty yards behind. "I saw dust on our back trail, the Shoshone are coming after the captives. They will be too busy trying to get away to worry about us."

"You would leave the others to the Shoshone?" asked an incredulous Big Horn. The two had been friends since childhood and he knew Spotted Elk to be an unscrupulous and vicious warrior, capable of anything to achieve his purposes, but to let the rest of the men of their war party possibly die to aid his escape? He had never turned on his own people before. If they did this and the others lived, they could never return to their village, they would be cast out. Big Horn shook his head, looked at the trail ahead, and knew his choice was already made. His friend had always succeeded, even in wrongdoing, and would probably succeed now. Besides, he had long wanted to have a rifle like the white men. He would be a great warrior if he only had a rifle, and this trade would make that possible. And it has ever been the way of evil doers, always believing they would be successful and would not be caught nor have to pay the price for their betrayal, and the rewards were always worth the risk.

He looked at his friend, "You said Charbonneau will give you two rifles, one for me?"

"Yes my friend, we always share, do we not?" questioned Spotted Elk.

Big Horn breathed deep, resigning himself to the deed, thinking only about his new rifle and how he would be a great warrior as he always dreamed he would. "Yes, we will do this," he answered.

Big Horn and Spotted Elk were the scouts, riding well ahead of the war party, but as the trail dropped from the mountain, dusk was settling into the valley and they chose the site for the camp then moved into the trees to wait for the others. The leader, *Cheshakhadakhi,* nodded as he came close, reined up and slid down from his mount. He spoke to the others, assigning tasks and captives. "Each one is to be tied, but also bound to her guard so they cannot flee, like the one that was killed," he glanced at Spotted Elk as his lip curled in a snarl. "We will have no others lost!"

The war leader chose four warriors for the captives, choosing men that were not closely allied with Spotted Elk or Big Horn. But that left them free and unhindered for their planned flight. But, they would have to separate the girl with the braids from her captor. They walked to the edge of the small stream, watering their horses and spoke softly as they stood holding the leads of the horses and stroked their back with handfuls of grass, rubbing them down as they talked over the backs of their mounts.

"How can we get her from Red Tail? He is a good warrior and light sleeper?" asked Big Horn.

"I will do that. You will get the horses, one for her also, and be ready there," he nodded his head toward the point of aspen that stretched into the valley.

Big Horn looked where Spotted Elk pointed, looked back at his friend, "You can do this?"

"Yes! I will do this. We will wait till the moon is high, then you get the horses, and I will get the girl. We will soon have our rifles, as I said!"

***

Orion held his stance, the uplifted sword above his head, the shield before him, as he stared down at the formidable lion. The lion did not move, neither did Orion, for they were forever stationed in the heavens above to watch over the people below. The star at the tip of his sword held the attention of Gabe as he lay beneath the long limb of the ponderosa. The branches thin with lone needles framing the image of the great hunter in the heavens.

Gabe remembered the time he and Pale Otter had looked at the constellation and she said, "That is our star! Every time I see that star, whether we are together or apart, I will think of you for you are my great hunter!" She would slip her hand in the crook of his arm and draw close, leaning her head on his shoulder and smiling, always smiling, as they stood together beneath the canopy of distant lanterns.

He sighed deeply, rolled from his blankets and stood, lifting his eyes to the moon. The scattered clouds made the gibbous night light play the childish game of peek-a-boo, but Gabe knew that could work to their advantage for the plan. He walked around their camp, thinking about the plan for the attack on the Hidatsa warriors and their captives. He had never fought the Hidatsa, but Shoots Running Buffalo said they were fierce warriors, yet he knew the danger for the captives. He believed they had already killed two, and would not hesitate to kill the others, and they were on a rescue mission, not just vengeance. If they were to wait for the other Shoshone and Shoots Buffalo to catch up and then attack, the raiders could possibly escape, and the captives would be lost.

He turned back to nudge the others awake, but Ezra and Cougar Woman had already risen, and Black Dog was sitting up. Wolf was at Gabe's side as he spoke, "We will take the horses, about a mile into the canyon there's a long ridge that comes down to the river. We can leave our horses there, split up and the camp is 'bout a half mile further."

They loaded their gear and started out. The gibbous moon standing high overhead, watching over them as they moved down the slope to cross the river. Gabe had spotted a likely crossing, the river only about fifty yards across and the gravelly bottom gave the horses good footing. The water was belly deep, but none of the horses had any difficulty with the crossing. In less than a quarter hour, they came to the timbered ridge where they were to leave the horses. The four moved quietly and tethered the animals by some juniper in a small clearing that offered some graze.

The four came together as Gabe strung his bow, using his bent knees to hold the risers as he bent the limbs back and notched the string. Black Dog had not seen the bow and frowned as he watched Gabe and his contortions to string the unusual weapon. Gabe spoke to Ezra, "I'm leavin' my rifle, but I'm takin' the two saddle pistols. We need to try to do this as quietly as possible, but, don't hesitate to shoot if need be."

Ezra shook his head, "I'm just takin' my pistol and war club. In the dark, I work better close up."

Cougar Woman and Black Dog were holding their bows, already strung, as they waited for the high sign to start. Gabe looked at them, "You three will take that trail," pointing to a thin trail that crested the ridge at a bit of a saddle, "I'm goin' down to the water's edge.

When you get over there, Ezra, you'll be next to the talus slope, and you two will be in the low brush on the flat." He looked from one to the other, "I reckon the guards will be at the trees next to the slope, and on the far edge, watching back up the canyon." He looked to Cougar Woman and Black Dog, "Leave the guards to me'n Black Buffalo, but if you can get in and cut loose the captives, then do it. But don't get in a hurry." He looked from one to the other, each one nodding their understanding. He looked to Ezra, "Give me a few minutes lead time 'fore you start, those rocks by the water ain't easy crossin'."

Ezra nodded and watched as Gabe turned away and crossed the slight rise at the end of the ridge and dropped over the edge of the river bank. The bank rose about forty or fifty feet above the river and held a smattering of brush that clung to the steep banks, but he and Wolf would stay near the water, letting the crashing water of the cascades mask his approach. He would allow what he guessed to be about a little less than a quarter hour before they would start their stalk. Once away from the trees and brush, their movements would have to be slow and stealthy, and stealth always took time.

15 / CLASH

Lean Wolf was instantly angered when he saw Red Tail unmoving, obviously asleep, and the captive girl gone. He kicked at the big warrior, but he rolled to the side, eyes open and staring at the canopy of quakies, his throat gaping open and a pool of blood behind his head and neck. Lean Wolf turned quickly, looking over the camp as he pulled his tomahawk from his belt and dropped into a warrior's crouch. No one moved, the dim light of early morning grey showed little but shadows. He barked, "HO! We've been attacked!!"

All the warriors rolled instantly to their feet, grabbing at weapons, searching the trees and the clearing for any threat. Those tethered to the captives jerked the girls to their feet and pulled them in front of them as shields. Lean Wolf shouted, "Big Horn! Spotted Elk! Find them!!" The other warriors scampered, scanning the tree line, and searching for tracks. A shout came from Walks Like a Dog, "Here! They went to their horses, dragging the captive girl!" He pointed to the trail that ducked around the trees and headed into the mountains.

"Big Nose, Lone Man, get your horses, go! If you find them soon, kill them! But if not, return! We need you against the Shoshone!" shouted Lean Wolf. He watched as the two warriors swung aboard their mounts and took off at a run, rounding the point of trees and assaulting the steep trail into the thick timber. He shook his head as he snarled, "Traitors!" He looked at the others, barked orders to gather the horses and get ready to leave. Some snatched pemmican or jerky from their packs, chewing as they worked to break camp and be ready to leave. Mumbling among the warriors was vehement, for the betrayal by their friends would also cost them. After Spotted Elk killed one captive and stole another, they were left with three captives and one already claimed by their leader. Little Frog and Smoke on Horse had been wounded, but not badly and were still able to ride and fight, but if the Shoshone sent a large party after them, it would be a difficult fight at best, and deadly at worst. And if Big Nose and Lone Man did not return, then it would be worse.

But Big Nose and Lone Man did return, but without Spotted Elk and Big Horn and the captive girl. "That trail climbs high, it would take two, three suns to catch them. They must have left in the middle of the night to be so far," explained Lone Man. "You said return if we did not catch them soon." He spoke to Lean Wolf, their war leader who showed his rage by his stare and clenched jaw. His lip curled and nostrils flared as he turned to the others, "Spotted Elk and Big Horn have betrayed us! They stole a captive and ran away! By our law they are exiles and should be killed at first sight!" The others shouted their war cries, shaking their clubs and lances in the air, kicking their horses to prance about and stir up a ruckus. Lean Wolf shook his lance over his head and waved to the others to follow as they started off at a canter.

By dusk, the mumbling and grumbling had subsided, but the anger still boiled underneath the usual staid countenances. The image of Red Tail as they buried him under the caved in bank still stirred their rage, knowing he had been killed by two of their own. The thought of betrayal was despicable to most, and knowing one they had followed and fought beside had betrayed them was an unheard of act by the Hidatsa, a people that were known for loyalty to one another and fierceness in battle as they fought side by side, always protecting one another.

As they made their camp, an undercurrent of distrust simmered, but each one stifled the thoughts as their duties were given by their leader Lean Wolf. Once again, men were assigned the task of guarding the captives by being tethered to them, and on this

night Bad Face and Smoke on Horse joined the number with Big Nose, as the guards for the young wom-
en. Little Frog and Lone Man were to be on guard for
the first half of the night, then would be relieved, but
both men were wary, not just of pursuing Shoshone,
but also their own.

***

The trail around the point stayed above the steep
shale that rose from the water, but at the far edge of
the point, Gabe and Wolf dropped down and through
the low growing juniper to start working their way
upstream. The rounded river donies, rocks that had
been tumbled and rounded by the fast-moving current at high water, made footing a little precarious,
but only for Gabe, Wolf had little difficulty picking his
way as he followed his friend. Along the water's edge,
Gabe had to stealthily pick his footing, often leaning
into the bank, and holding to the low juniper brush
or the many berry bushes. The choke cherry, service
berry and wild roses flourished on the steep bank,
and the currant bushes filled in the gaps, all making
Gabe's passage challenging.

It was a little less than a half-mile to his point of
exit from the river, every step a challenge to keep
from twisting an ankle or breaking other bones in
the unstable rocky footing. But he moved steadily,

Wolf close behind and the cut in the bank was marked by a small cluster of juniper trees that sided the little creek bed that came from the mountain behind the Hidatsa camp. Gabe sat down for a moment to catch his breath and position his weapons. His bow had been at his back and he brought it from his shoulder, nocked an arrow, and checked his pistols and blades. He took a deep breath, looked at Wolf and whispered, "Alright boy, here we go," and started up the cut.

There was just a trickle of water in the creek bed, but berry bushes and willows were abundant on both sides, giving some cover to Gabe and Wolf. Gabe was on his belly, inching his way in the shadows of the willows, Wolf directly behind. He twisted to look at the moon and clouds, trying to use the darker times when the face of the moon was covered, as he made his stalk. He continually watched the trees at the rise of the hill's low ridge, believing that to be the best location for a guard, but he scanned the willows and bushes at every move. For about a half hour, he bellied forward to cover the hundred yards from the river bank to the tree line. He moved an arm, the opposite leg, and slowly lifted his body to inch forward, watching the trees for movement.

When the moon slid from behind a cloud and cast its blue light round about, Gabe stopped, watching the trees. There! Movement at the base of the nearest juniper, directly in front of him, a solitary guard that had grown restless, moved his leg and was spotted by

Gabe. It is the slightest movement that gives one away, but as Gabe looked, he knew he could not approach the guard from this position, for his own movement would give his position away to the guard. He slowly turned to look through the brush, across the small creek bottom, and picked his path. Slowly pushing aside the lower branches of the currant bush, he bellied through the grass and the trickle of water, emerging on the far side beneath the willows. He paused, searching the campsite, then the trail and talus slope for any sign of Ezra and Cougar Woman, but saw nothing. He inched forward, keeping the brush between him and the guard, but knew he was more exposed to the rest of the camp but hopefully they were asleep.

He watched the guard, saw no movement, then the man stood and walked back to the trees, returned, and went over the slight rise of the ridge, probably to relieve himself. But that move gave Gabe the opportunity he needed. He slowly rose, catfooted toward the trees, and waited for the guard's return. A short moment later, the guard returned and settled back into his chosen position, to lean against the tree. Once Gabe saw him relax, he moved forward, reached around the tree, and cupped his hand over the guard's mouth and slit his throat. The guard kicked and struggled, but just for a short moment, then relaxed in death. Gabe motioned Wolf to his side, and they started through the trees, searching for the captives.

***

Ezra allowed Gabe the short lead time, then started on the trail over the saddle of the ridge. Cougar Woman and Black Dog followed, but once at the bottom and at the edge of the long flat, Cougar Woman and Black Dog separated, and watching the moon and the clouds, slowly moved when the moon was covered, always at a crawl and staying as low as possible, using the sage and rabbit brush for cover. As they neared some sage, both cut several thick branches to use as cover, for their approach would be in the open with little other brush to shield their approach.

Ezra hugged the steep talus slope, choosing every hump, contour, and tree or shrub for cover. He had removed his tunic, and carried his war club across his chest, always at the ready. His pistol weighed heavy in his belt, his tomahawk and knife close to hand at his hips. There was the line of trees that hugged the end of the talus and shielded him from the camp, but he took advantage of every shadow, every bush, and moved as quiet as a lynx on the hunt. His moccasined feet padded silently as he picked his steps carefully, then dropped behind a low growing juniper as he neared the camp. He was on one knee, unmoving, as he searched the entire camp and the edge and tree line for the guard. He peered into the deep shadows, searching, watching, and slowly began to make out the form of a man standing, leaning against the white bark of an aspen. He had chosen the nearest tree, unmindful of how the bark would make him noticeable, thinking only of comfort during his long watch. He did not think of someone watching him, for he was the watcher, looking for those that might attack the camp or those within the camp that might try to flee. But that assumption was his downfall.

Ezra watched the leaning man, saw him slowly slide down the tree trunk and sit at its base, leaning back against the smooth trunk. Ezra scanned the area around, saw no easy approach, and knew he would be exposed if he started for the man. He could only hope the guard was snoozing as he started from his cover. Staying close to the trees and brush, no quick moves, Ezra glanced occasionally to the camp, and moved toward the guard. He hung the war club at his back, slipped his knife from the scabbard at his waist, and dropped into a low crouch as he came from behind the brush. Still he moved slowly, feeling his steps, and was within striking distance when the guard came awake, looked up at the knife flashing in the moonlight, and started to shout, emitting a gurgling cry as the knife slipped between his ribs and Ezra's hand covered his mouth. But the guard was strong and kicked, jerked his face to the side and opened his mouth to shout, but Ezra brought the knife from the man's ribs to his throat as they struggled, and the man crashed to the side, whimpering. Ezra twisted around, came to his feet as he turned, and saw several forms starting to rise.

He grabbed his pistol, cocking the hammer as it came from his belt and leveled it at the nearest warrior that was drawing his bow with an arrow, and fired. The blast split the night, echoing across the canyon, and those that had not moved, rolled quickly from their blankets, grabbing for weapons.

Gabe had heard the movement from the other side of the camp, knew Ezra was probably at that edge, and turned his attention to the sleeping forms. The roar of the pistol startled him, but he pulled one of his saddle pistols, bringing one hammer to full cock, keeping the bow in his left hand. He chose a target who was standing with his bow, searching for an intruder in the direction of the first shot, and fired. The pistol bucked, spat fire into the darkness, and sent the lead missile into the warrior's chest, knocking him to his knees and sending the arrow clattering among the trees.

Gabe jammed the pistol back into his belt and drew the arrow back, let it fly and saw it take another warrior high on his chest. He quickly nocked another arrow as he searched for a raider, saw a man beside a captive, but before he could let the arrow go, Wolf lunged at the man's throat, sunk his teeth in his neck and rode him to the ground, ripping the man's throat from his neck, spewing blood and he tore it free. The girl that was tethered to the man, struggled against her tether, trying to get free of the black wolf, but Wolf dropped into his attack stance, turning his back on the girl, guarding her from any attackers.

Gabe slipped the bow over his back and lifted the pistol, cocking the second hammer and started toward the girl, searching the camp for others. Another Hidatsa warrior rose, a lance coming up and back as he readied a throw, but an arrow came from the edge of the trees, impaling itself in the man's neck. The warrior grabbed at the shaft as his knees buckled and he fell to the ground, both hands gripping at the arrow as death wrapped its cloak around him.

Ezra lifted the war club from his back and started toward the rising Hidatsa. He screamed his war cry and started swinging. The raiders were startled by the image of the black man before them, he was a shadow of fury, a creature from the nether world, half man, half bull buffalo, the whites of his eyes and teeth showing in the darkness, as he waded into the middle of them. His first blow caught a surprised warrior with the halberd blade as it was buried in his neck, almost decapitating him. Ezra jerked it free as the man fell, and on his back swing, cut the legs from another, dropping him to his side, but Ezra used the sharpened tip of the ironwood war club and pierced the Hidatsa warrior's throat with death.

Ezra turned to face the others just in time to see an arrow loosed toward him, he jumped up and to the side, but the arrow pierced his thigh. He dropped to his feet, looked down at the arrow protruding from his thigh, glowered at the shooter and lunged toward him as he tried to nock another arrow, but the war club struck his arm, breaking it just above the elbow, then Ezra whirled around, and clubbed the man's head, caving it in and making his eye pop out on his cheek, just before he fell in death. Ezra spun around, searching for another target, felt the pain in his leg, but did his best to ignore it. He spotted another warrior, tethered to a girl, and slipped the pistol from his belt, twisted the barrels to the second one, cocked the hammer and lifted the muzzle. The warrior was looking at Gabe and trying to lift his tomahawk, but the girl was fighting him. He stepped back just as Ezra leveled the pistol and fired. The bullet punctured through his ribs under his arm, piercing his heart and bringing instant death. The man crumpled to the ground, but the girl stood, watching as he fell.

Gabe started for the tethered girl, but in his rush, a stone rolled underfoot, and as he fought for balance, he tripped on a root and fell. He rolled to the side, starting to rise, but an Hidatsa was charging with a lance. Gabe dug for a pistol but was startled when a war cry pierced the dark and another form seemed to come flying from the brush and struck the charging Hidatsa, burying a tomahawk in his head, almost splitting it in two. Cougar Woman stood, looked at a wide-eyed Gabe, "Are you just going to lie there or are you going to fight?"

Gabe scrambled to his feet as Cougar Woman cut the captive free. The girl pointed out the other captives, "There, and there!" and Cougar Woman went to one and Gabe to the other. The nearest warrior to Cougar Woman was watching Ezra, spellbound by the black beast that looked every bit like the muscled bulls of the buffalo, until a knife split his ribs from behind. He arched his back, turned to look at the Shoshone warrior that struck him and was surprised to see Cougar Woman. He slowly shook his head as his legs gave way and he crumpled in death. Cougar Woman quickly cut through the tether and the rawhide that bound the girl's hands together. "I am Cougar Woman of the Shoshone!" she declared as she motioned to the others, "These are our friends."

Black Dog had killed one when the warriors fled in a panic from the raging wolf, and with a well-placed arrow at the onset of the fight, he took down one of the panicked warriors. But the numbers killed by Ezra, Gabe, and Cougar Woman accounted for the rest. As they gathered the girls together, one known as Squirrel explained, "The one called Spotted Elk killed White Fox and stole Sacajawea. Another went with him, Big Horn. These," motioning to the dead Hidatsa, "were very mad when that happened."

"When did they take Sacajawea?" asked Cougar Woman.

"In the night, before yesterday. When the scouts came back, they said they were too far gone to catch." She dropped her eyes, and added quietly, "Spotted Elk will kill her when he grows tired of her."

Both Gabe and Ezra heard her words, looked at one another and knew there was little chance of pursuing the renegades and recovering the girl. That was the first that Gabe noticed the arrow protruding from Ezra's thigh, and he looked up at his friend, "Uh, you know you have an arrow in your leg?"

Ezra looked down, back at Gabe, "I *thought* somethin' bit me!"

16 / LIMP

Cougar Woman took charge of tending the wound of Ezra. She sent Gabe and Black Dog for the horses and when they returned, she tasked them with disposing of the bodies of the Hidatsa. She had the girls fetching plants and building a fire, using some of the gear of the vanquished to make Ezra comfortable. He rather enjoyed the attention, but the arrow was awkward and painful. Fortunately, the arrowhead had punched through the thick thigh and Cougar Woman started cutting the head and fletching off, over the moans and groans of Ezra.

"Are you going to make that noise all the time?" she asked, adjusting her position to give better access to the point of the shaft and head.

"I ain't 'makin' noise, I'm just gettin' comfortable!" declared Ezra, rolling away from his nurse, giving her clearance to work.

The girls returned with Goldenrod and Arrowleaf to be made into a balm and Cougar Woman instructed, "Use some aspen bark, make a bowl, put in water, and the plants. When it boils, pour out most of the water and make a balm of the rest."

The girls, Squirrel and Running Rabbit, nodded and went to the fire while the third girl took one of the knives taken from the Hidatsa and went to the quakies for some bark. Within a short while, the ointment was ready, and Cougar Woman had cleaned the wound, shoved the arrow shaft out, and had bandages, made from a blanket of the raiders, ready to apply. She patted on the poultice and strapped the bandage on with rawhide strips and looked to Ezra for his response.

Ezra looked down at the bandage that circled his thigh, then up to Cougar Woman, and said, "That's good. That stuff you put on, made it feel better already." He sat up, looking around for Gabe and Black Dog, saw the two coming toward them and started to get up. He winced and sat back down, frowning at Cougar Woman, "Ow! What'd you do to me?"

Cougar Woman stood, shaking her head, "I fixed you. If you want to complain, tell the Hidatsa about it!" She looked at him, "If you are Shoshone as you claim, you will get up and move like a warrior. If you do not, it will get stiff and hurt even more."

As Gabe came near to give his friend a hand, Ezra looked up at him, "You sure have a bossy woman there, my friend."

Gabe chuckled, glanced back at Cougar Woman who was smiling at the two and shook his head. "What makes you think she's my woman?"

Ezra frowned, glaring at his friend as he struggled up, then grunting he added, "Maybe you don't know it, but everybody else does."

They were just getting ready to have some hot food when Shoots Running Buffalo and the other Shoshone rode up to the camp. He slipped down, walked to the group by the fire, and was happily greeted by the three girls. He looked to Gabe and Ezra and asked, "Where are the Hidatsa?"

Gabe pointed to the mound at the bottom of the talus slope where they used the rock and dirt from the slide to cover the bodies. "We couldn't wait. They had already killed one of the girls, White Fox, but we thought they'd killed two, and that the two wounded raiders had died. So we attacked in the night, and Squirrel there told us that one of their own had killed the girl and stolen your brother's girl, Sacajawea. They left the night before, an' she," nodding toward Squirrel, "said she can show you where the two warriors who stole her left the others. But I think they're long gone."

Shoots motioned to the others to get down, then looked around at those by the fire, "And you," nodding to Gabe and the others, "attacked the band and killed them all?"

"Ummhmm, that's about it," answered Gabe. "But Ezra there took an arrow in his thigh."

Shoots sat down near Gabe, turned to look at him, "I must go after those that took the girl."

"I figgered you'd say that, but I need to take my friend back to his woman."

Shoots nodded, understanding, "I will take two or three with me, if you will lead the others back to the encampment."

"We can do that. We were just havin' us a bite to eat, an' we'll start back. It's a ways back on the trail 'fore we come to the place where the others took off. Squirrel said the scouts said it was a mighty steep trail and hard goin'," explained Gabe.

"I think I know the place, but I will talk to Squirrel. If it is the same, I know a different trail we can take to save some time," suggested Shoots.

***

It was a two-day ride back to the encampment, and they stopped several times to rest and change the bandages on Ezra's leg. Shoots Running Buffalo and three others separated from the band at the place he said would take them over the mountains and maybe save time in their pursuit of the raiders. When Gabe and company rode into camp, Black Dog and the other warriors took the girls to the camp of their people and Gabe, Ezra, and Cougar Woman were greeted by Dove, who quickly noticed the bandage and helped Ezra to the ground. He leaned on Dove as they went into the tipi, and Gabe took the horses into the trees where they had made a small corral of brush and poles to keep their horses.

Before they parted, Cougar Woman spoke to Gabe, "I will go to the lodge of my father and tell of our journey. I will return soon."

Gabe smiled, nodded, and said, "I'll be waitin'."

***

It was a somber faced Cougar Woman who returned in the early evening. She sat down on the log near Gabe, hung her head and sat quiet, until Gabe asked, "What's wrong? Bad news?"

"Little Mountain has been talking a lot. Demanding to be made war leader over me, but the chiefs refused. He will not be satisfied until it is settled," she explained.

"Does that mean you'll have to fight him?" asked Gabe.

"Yes, there is no other way."

"I don't doubt that you can win over him."

"But I do not want to kill him. He has been a friend most of my life." She shook her head as she looked at Gabe, "But he cannot stand it that I am a leader and he is not. We have always competed since we were young. He is a good warrior, but a poor leader. Because he is so big, he thinks he can just use his strength anytime. But the rest of the warriors cannot fight like that." She was obviously exasperated, as is common when others choose to act in such a way that rationale is set aside because of blind ambition and jealousy.

"Have you ever had a fight such as this?"

"No. It has not been necessary; others have seen me fight our enemies and chose to make me leader. I do not want to fight one of our own."

Gabe thought a few moments, deliberating an idea that had taken form in his mind. He looked at Cougar Woman, head hanging, dejected, concerned as she was, and decided. "Could I show you some ways to use Little Mountain's size against him? Ways that you could use in the fight?"

Cougar Woman frowned, "Use his weight against him? You could do that?"

"You saw him after we 'bumped' into each other in the woods. And you also noticed there was not a mark on me. That is what I can show you, if you are willing."

As they talked, Ezra hobbled from the tipi and joined them at the fire, Dove sitting close beside him. Gabe looked at his friends, then at Dove, "So, you think he's gonna be alright?"

Dove smiled, "Cougar Woman did very well when she took care of my man. He will be good soon." She lay her hand gently on his leg and bandage, smiled up at Ezra and added, "As long as he quits complaining. If not, it might take a long time for him to heal!" she cautioned, smiling, and everyone understanding as they laughed together.

Ezra looked at Cougar Woman and Gabe, "So, what's with you two. You act like somethin's wrong."

Gabe quickly explained about Little Mountain and added, "So, I thought I'd show her a few ways to use his weight and size against him."

Ezra let a slow smile paint his face, then glanced from Cougar Woman to Dove and said, "That'll be somethin' to see." He looked back at Gabe, "Think you can show her 'nuff 'fore time comes?"

"I think so, there's a few moves that I used on him that worked quite well, so, prob'ly." He looked at Cougar Woman, "Class begins first thing in the mornin'. We'll go back in the trees yonder. I saw a nice grassy clearing back in there a ways that'll do just fine."

17 / TRAINING

The air was cool, and the morning sky showed a pink canopy blending with the promised blue as the two friends walked to the clearing. Gabe was explaining the basics of the Akiyama Yoshin-ryustyle of Jujutsu as he learned them when visiting England with his father. At the clearing, Gabe patiently showed just four of the many strategic points that would cause considerable pain when struck with a partially clenched fist, using the extended knuckles as the weapon. The first was the temple, second the ribs at the side of the sternum, the lower belly, and the inside of the knee, just above the joint. "For this last one, use the side of your foot, striking down, like this," demonstrating as he spoke.

He repeated each of the moves, suggested she try, and she immediately demonstrated her skill and quick learning. They practiced using those points as they moved, and she repeatedly struck Gabe accurately, pulling her punches so as not to injure. "I can see where these would be very painful," she said as she pulled back from using her foot against his knee. Gabe had gone to the ground, holding his knee and shaking his head as he looked up at his student.

Cougar Woman grinned, stepped back, "But how do these use his strength and size against him?"

As Gabe rose, he breathed deep, looking at the woman, "These don't. Now I'll show you about those moves. The first one I call a hip roll," and he demonstrated stepping close, spinning and catching the assailant around the waist and back and pushing against him with his own hip, then rolling the assailant over his hip. He kept Cougar Woman from dropping to the ground, helped her upright and let her try. Again, she was a quick learner, and after three attempts, each one successful, she said, "And another?"

Gabe grinned, "Alright, this one I call a leg sweep. But all the moves are based on getting your opponent off-balance. Once that is done, you have the advantage." As he demonstrated, he added, "It's what some call, 'to push when pulled, to pull when pushed.' Using their momentum against them." He demonstrated the movement, then the leg sweep, then combined the moves. They practiced together for most of the morning until Ezra and Dove came to watch.

"So, Ezra, how 'bout letting Cougar Woman practice with you?" suggested Gabe.

"What makes you think I want to get thrown around?" he wailed, good naturedly.

"You don't know what she's learned nor what she will try, and you'll go easy on her. It'll be good practice."

"I'll go easy on her, but will she go easy on me? I still have this wound!" he added, pointing at the bandage on his leg.

Cougar Woman stepped closer and said, "I will not hurt you little man," smiling.

"Little man?! Alright girl," growled Ezra, struggling to his feet.

As the two opponents approached one another, both in a fighter's crouch and circling one another, Ezra showed no favoritism to his wounded leg, but focused on Cougar Woman. He leaned forward, feinting a charge, but Cougar Woman moved quickly before he could regain his balance, and threw him over her hip, but held on so he would not crash to the ground, injuring his wound. She lowered him to the ground and Ezra looked up from his back, "That was good!" She helped him to his feet, and they circled again. She darted about, showing a charge, withdrawing, and a quick move that would have broken Ezra's leg if she hadn't pulled her strike. A few moment's more and she had attempted most of the moves she learned, then they both relaxed, and walked to the grassy shade where Dove and Gabe waited.

Wolf lay beside the cradle board, watching over the babe, as Ezra sat with Dove and Cougar Woman seated herself beside Gabe. "You did well, now with a couple days practice, I think you can put it to use when you go against Little Mountain," suggested Gabe as he looked at Cougar Woman. He glanced at Ezra, "Don't you think so?" he asked.

"Uh, yeah. After what she just showed me, and with some practice, I wouldn't want to get into it with her," declared Ezra, glancing from Cougar Woman to Dove.

Dove looked at Cougar Woman, "This is the last day of the Sun Dance. We should go."

Cougar Woman nodded, looked at the men and asked, "Will you go with us?"

"Sure, we'll go. It would be good to see the dance I've heard so much about," answered Gabe, looking from Cougar to Ezra and Dove.

***

In the midst of the crowd stood a circular structure. A tall center pole, surrounded by twelve poles, each connected to the center pole by a braided rawhide rope. The outside poles hand been interlaced with branches to provide a wall that protected the dancers. The crowd was seated around the structure, some standing further back, and a slight slope offered space for others. Gabe and company took a place on the slope, overlooking the compound. Once seated, Gabe asked Cougar Woman, "So, tell me about this, what are they doing," nodding to the dancers, "and why?"

"Long ago, our chief, *Ohamagwaya*, Yellow Hand, had a vision. He went on a quest for *bcx*, power. He took a grey painted buffalo robe and had a vision of a man that told him what to do. You can see at the entrance, there is a buffalo hide, and inside at the far edge, is an eagle. They are to give the dancers power as they dance and pray to the sun for the answer to their prayers. They dance, blow the whistles, to seek blessings and good for themselves, the people and the land. When they approach the pole the first day, they are painted white, but the rest of the time they are painted many colors."

Gabe was listening intently, watching the dancers and the people, but when Cougar Woman paused, he asked, "But now, there are no drums, why?"

Cougar Woman smiled, "They have been dancing for almost four days, without water, food, and very little rest. When they dance, they start each day by rubbing their talisman on their wrists on the center pole, and the bells at their ankles keep them moving, forward and back, throughout the day. The drums stop after three days, and on the fourth or last day, today, most are exhausted and drop, those that can still move will leave the circle."

"Then what, is that all?" asked Ezra, looking at Cougar Woman and Dove.

"No," she pointed to the crowd that moved about, "there are several cookfires and food is prepared for a great feast. Those that danced and their families will give away gifts, sometimes all they own, to show their sincerity in their prayers."

Gabe had been watching the last of the dancers and saw a familiar figure stagger from the arbor, he frowned and nodded toward the man, then asked, "Is that Snake Eater?"

Cougar Woman looked, smiled, "Yes, he was one of the dancers."

Gabe looked at her again, "Did Little Mountain dance also?"

She shook her head, "No, he has never danced. He does not believe in the power of the dance."

They sat together, enjoying the moment, and watching the activity of the crowd. Gabe leaned back on his elbows, crossed his legs at the ankles and spoke to Ezra, "Say, you remember the dance of the Arapaho, didn't they call that the Sun Dance?"

Ezra frowned, looked at his friend, "Yeah, they did. Come to think of it, theirs *was* similar to this one. They had a lot of ceremony leadin' up to it, the shamans and everything doin' the cleansing sweat baths and such, then they got pretty involved in building the arbor, too."

"And they said the Cheyenne did much the same, didn't they?"

Ezra frowned again, "Ummhmm, they did at that."

Cougar Woman spoke up, "I have heard the Black-foot and the Ute also have a dance like this one. But I think ours goes back further. *Ohamagwaya,* Yellow Hand, was a chief and a shaman. His vision came to him on the mountain when he was alone. It is his vision that we follow, not the ways of the other tribes."

"So, you think the Great Spirit might give the same vision to different leaders or shamans of different tribes?" asked Gabe.

Cougar Woman thought about it, looked to Dove and then at Gabe, "How is our *Boha,* or Great Spirit different than your God?"

"Well, I suppose, in many ways. But what you believe about the Great Spirit is similar to what we know about our God."

"So, would your God tell more than one person the same thing?"

Gabe grinned, looked at Cougar Woman, "Yes, He has. But, when He does, what He tells each one is the same. They may relate it a little differently, but it is still the same. He did that when He gave us the Bible. The first four books of the New Testament tell the same story, but from different perspectives, but all agree."

"So, our *Boha, our Father,* or Great Spirit could do the same," stated Cougar Woman.

"But why is each one so different?" asked Gabe.

Cougar Woman frowned, shook her head, "I do not know, for I am not a *boha grande*, or shaman." She gave a firm nod and turned away to show the conversation about that subject was finished. Gabe shook his head as he grinned, glanced at Ezra who shrugged and grinned, and both men turned their attention to the preparations for the feast.

It was a joyous feast that later broke into a round dance, where men and women danced to the cadence of the big drums, drums that had six or more beating the cadence. The women appeared in fanciful garb, long laces hanging from the sleeves to the ground, intricate bead and quill work forming meaningful designs. Most dancers had a feather fan or decorated war shield as they danced, adding to the rhythmic steps that took them around the circle. Gabe looked at Cougar Woman, "Why do you not dance?"

"I am a war leader, it is not right," she answered simply, then glanced at Dove, who had been covered with a blanket wrapped about her shoulders as she carried the cradle board with the child before her. But now, Dove stood, lowered the blanket to reveal a beautiful white buckskin dress with bead work that covered her chest, and long broad strips of quillwork that cascaded from her shoulders to the hem. The long fringe, holding bright blue tufts of rabbit fur to match the beads, hung near the ground. Her high-topped moccasins were white and beaded like her dress, and she reached into the folds of the blanket and brought out a matching tunic which she held out to Ezra.

Ezra's eyes grew wide as he slowly stood and accepted the tunic. It too was beaded and fringed, and as Ezra slipped it over his muscled frame, his chest bulged under and showed the black of his skin at the deep cut neck. Dove handed him matching moccasins which he quickly pulled on, and Dove pushed the cradle board toward Cougar Woman. When they stood together, they were a striking couple, both smiling broadly, and they quickly turned and joined the dancers.

As the activities began to subside, Cougar Woman slung the cradle board on her back and she and Gabe started for the tipi. They waved at the dancers, got a nod of approval, and walked off into the darkness. They enjoyed the quiet of the night, looking up at the stars and appreciating the cool evening breeze. Most of the way, they walked in silence, until Gabe reached down to take Cougar's hand. She accepted his clasp and asked, "What will you do after the encampment? Will you return with the village of your friends?"

"It is my village as well. We have a cabin in the mountains where the village is camped, and we will return there." He paused as he looked at her, "And what about you?"

"I have not thought much about anything past the bout with Little Mountain," she sighed heavily, "If I lose and live, I will no longer be a war leader and will lose much in stature with my people. But if I win, there will still be conflict with Little Mountain."

"But why? I thought once he was defeated that would be the end of it."

She walked a moment in silence, then stopped and turned to look at Gabe, "He has been talking and recruiting followers. He has said I am not loyal to my people and I would rather be with you than my own people."

Gabe frowned, thought about it a moment, then with his hands at the sides of her shoulders he asked, "And what do you say to that?"

"I am loyal to my people, I have always been loyal and always will, but you have a great pull on me. When I am not with you, I find myself thinking of you and looking for you and wanting to be with you."

Gabe let a slow smile split his face as he slowly pulled Cougar Woman close and wrapped his arms around her as he spoke softly, "It is the same with me."

They held the embrace a long moment, then slowly drew away to look at one another, "What do we do?" asked Cougar Woman.

Gabe smiled, "What do most couples do when they want to be together always?"

Cougar Woman smiled, "A joining ceremony?"

18 / BOUT

They met up as they were returning from their morning time with the Lord, each to his own chosen sanctuary, and Ezra saw a troubled look on Gabe's face. "What is it, my friend?" he asked.

Gabe frowned as he looked at Ezra, "What do you mean?"

"Oh, come on, I can read you easier than the weather, something's goin' on with you. Is it Cougar Woman?"

Gabe turned quickly to look at his friend, "Is it that obvious?"

"Yeah, but I thought I'd see you smilin', not lookin' all grumpy an' such."

Gabe motioned for them to sit on a long grey log, the remnant of some long-ago blowdown, then leaned forward, elbows on his knees and face in his hands. "Every time I get to thinkin' 'bout Cougar Woman and maybe taking her home with us, the image of Pale Otter comes to mind." He paused, sat back and looked at his friend, "I feel like I'm betraying Otter or something, but it's been a year since she passed. But . . . I don't know, it's tearin' me up inside. When I think of Cougar Woman goin' against that ape, Little Mountain, I wanna go after him and tear him apart. Or the idea of leavin' here without her, just doesn't sit well either!"

Ezra waited a moment, picked up a twig at their feet and tossed it aside then turned to look at his friend. "I don't need to tell you that what you're feelin' is natural, you already know that. But from all you've said, you don't have much choice!"

Gabe frowned and looked at his friend, "I don't?"

"Nope! The way I see it that mischievous son of Aphrodite, old Cupid himself, done stuck you full of those golden arrows!"

Gabe shook his head, "The last thing I expected of you was to refer to some ancient Greek mythology. But . . . maybe you're right." He stood, looked at his friend, "Let's go get us somethin' to eat!"

"I'm all for that!"

***

Dove and Cougar Woman were busy at the fire preparing the food for the first meal of the day. They had camas roots and cattail roots roasting in the coals, the coffee pot was dancing on the flat rock beside the flames, and strips of fresh venison were sizzling in the pan. Dove had earlier put some corn bread in the dutch oven that sat beside the fire, covered with hot coals. The women looked up as Gabe and Ezra walked into the camp. Although their lodge was a part of the encampment of the village, it was set back nearer the trees and afforded them some privacy. Gabe grabbed up the coffee pot and two cups, handed one to Ezra as he sat down and poured it full of the steaming brew. He filled his cup, sat the pot down and joined Ezra on the log.

"This looks like quite a feast, especially for breakfast!" observed Gabe.

The women looked at one another, and Cougar Woman spoke softly, "I must fight today."

The unspoken thoughts filled everyone's mind, thoughts of the possibility of the worst outcome, that Cougar Woman could be killed, or seriously injured, and that this was the last day of the encampment and they might go their separate ways. Gabe dropped his eyes, sighed heavily, and looked back, "We could just leave now, forget about the fight," he suggested, although he knew that would not happen.

"I cannot bring shame on my family, I must fight."

"But what kind of a man does not protect his woman?"

At the mention of 'his woman', both women looked at Gabe, eyes wide and brows lifted, "Your woman?" asked Dove.

"Yeah, *my* woman!"

Cougar Woman smiled and moved around the fire to sit beside Gabe, "You have protected me. Against the Blackfoot and the Hidatsa when we were facing our enemies. But, I am not a woman that must be protected. I am a warrior that will walk beside her man and fight alongside him against our enemies." She paused as she reached for Gabe's hand, "But I ask you to be there for me as I fight this man that would take my place among my people. It is not his to take, it is mine to give."

Gabe reached around Cougar Woman to draw her close and she lay her head on his shoulder, reaching her arm around him. They savored the moment for a short while, until Ezra broke the mood with, "Hey, breakfast is ready! Let's eat!"

***

Little Weasel was an impressive figure. The chief of the band of *Tukkutikka,* stood with a stoic expression, looking like he was the one going into battle. A bone breast plate covered his chest, two thick braids hung over his shoulders, and the braided topknot held four notched feathers. His broad brow showed few wrinkles, though the black hair showed grey at the temples. His muscular arms bulged, one held an engraved silver band, and tattoos covered the shoulder and other upper arm. His breechcloth was painted, and his fringed leggings had a narrow band of beadwork the full length of both legs. The toes of his moccasins showed similar beadwork. His arms were folded across his chest and his hands held two knives and two tomahawks.

The crowd had gathered with a sizable group to one side where Little Mountain seemed to be holding court. He was speaking animatedly, gesturing to those around him, and toward the far side of the crowd where Cougar Woman stood with her father and mother, Two Horses and Pretty Cloud. Gabe, Ezra and Grey Dove stood near, but separate.

Little Weasel stepped forward and spoke, "*Doyakukubichi' Wa'ipi,* Cougar Woman, Little Mountain, come," and motioned to the space before him.

The summoned warriors stepped forward, standing near one another, and facing the chief. The difference in size was immediately obvious, Little Mountain was bigger by any measurement, and he tried to bull his way forward, but Cougar Woman held her ground, refusing to give way. The glare from the chief stopped Little Mountain, and the chief spoke, "This is a challenge for war leader. This goes until one yields or one dies." He pushed his way between them, shoving each one aside. He glared at the onlookers, motioned them back and stepped to the center of the circle of villagers. The chief turned to face Cougar Woman and Little Mountain, held out the tomahawks toward Cougar Woman, "Choose!"

Cougar gave a quick look at the weapons, chose one and reached for it. The chief released his grip, then handed the other to Little Mountain. He held the knives before him and looked at Little Mountain, "Choose." The big warrior snatched a knife and stepped back as the chief handed the other to Cougar Woman. He looked from one to the other, walked to the edge of the circle and looked at each one again, then with a quick motion downward, the opponents started to the center of the circle.

It began with both warriors side stepping, cautiously crossing one foot over the other, staying low in a crouch, staring at one another as they moved around the circle. Little Mountain rolled his shoulders back, pushing out his chest, and growled, "You are nothing! I will cut you into pieces and feed you to the wolves!"

Cougar Woman acted as if she didn't hear him, said nothing, moved with measured steps and breathing, watching. Little Mountain lunged forward, but it was just a feint, and quickly stepped back. Cougar Woman anticipated his lunge, made a slight and almost unnoticeable move to the side and showed no fear as they resumed their circling. Little Mountain swept his knife and hawk side to side, as if he were cutting and hacking at her body, but she watched his eyes. She knew Little Mountain as an impatient bully who believed his bulk and muscle were all that was needed to vanquish any enemy and she anticipated his move when he lunged, arms wide, expecting to wrap her up in his arms and throw her.

As he came near, she ducked under his outstretched arm that held the knife, swiped at his leg with her knife, then spun around, slipping her arm around his bulk and lifted her hip to throw him to his back. The big bulk smashed down on his back, knocking the wind from him and his shock showed with his wide eyes that saw only blue sky and white clouds. He gasped for air, and rolled to his belly to push himself up, but Cougar had stepped behind him, and as he rose, looking side to side, he felt a searing pain as Cougar Woman sliced his back from shoulder to hip. But she did not drive the knife deep, wanting only to cut and make him bleed.

As Little Mountain roared and spun around, Cougar Woman ran the opposite direction around the circle, making the man turn totally around and be off balance as his own legs were tangled. Cougar Woman charged him but kicked up and struck him in the chest with both feet, knocking him to his back. The big man roared again as both warriors came to their feet, but now the Mountain was wary, and dropped into his crouch, snarling at her as the corner of his lip lifted and his nostrils flared, eyes squinted, and growled, "You cannot stand and fight! You're too weak! You're not a warrior, you are nothing but a woman!"

But Cougar Woman was too smart to be baited by his insults and feinted a charge that caused Little Mountain to shift his weight to the side, and Cougar flew past, cutting his upper arm as she passed. Blood streamed from the cut, but Little Mountain ignored the wound and charged the woman, determined to crush her or cut her. As he came, Cougar tossed her tomahawk aside, and the move surprised her attacker who glanced at the hawk too late, as Cougar ducked under his arm again, spun and cut his back shoulder to hip in one quick swipe. Now his back was marked by a big "X" that bloodied his entire back.

As Gabe watched the bout he was reminded of the attacks of wolves when they hound a buffalo, one striking while another attacks from behind, one always hounding while another draws attention. But Cougar Woman was doing the work of an entire pack, attacking, wounding, avoiding, striking, and always harassing.

Now Cougar Woman stood, holding only the knife, grinning at her opponent who was showing his frustration and aggravation. He had not laid a hand on her, but she had repeatedly dropped him and cut him. She knew he was becoming desperate and would be more careless yet determined. She moved closer, taunting him, waiting for him to reach out, but he surprised her with a feint that she responded to, and then grabbed her arms and threw her to the ground. Before she could twist away, he flopped his bulk on her, then straddled her, snarling, "Now! You will taste the blade of a warrior!" But in his anticipated victory, he had failed to pin her arms to her side and as he lifted his knife she slapped both open hands to his ears, followed by a quick knuckle punch at the base of his nose. The slap hurt his eardrums, possibly breaking them, and the punch drove his nose bone into his head, splattering the protuberance over his face, splashing blood on his jowls and chin and on Cougar Woman. The man was startled and hurt and when Cougar Woman bucked, he rolled to the side as she squirmed out from under him.

As she rose, she grabbed her knife and stood to the side, waiting for him to get to his feet. Even wounded and bloody as he was, he rose, quickly searched for his weapons which had been dropped when he grabbed at his ears, turned away from Cougar to reach for the hawk, but Cougar Woman appeared to fly through the air as she leaped toward him and came down with all her weight and might as she drove the side of her foot against his knee, buckling it and driving him to the ground. Little Mountain screamed in pain, grabbing at his leg as he fell to his side, pulling his leg up to his chest. It was bent at an awkward angle and was obviously broken just above the knee.

Cougar Woman stepped back, picked up the hawk and handed both the hawk and knife to Little Weasel. Everyone stood silent, the only sound coming from a whining and sobbing Little Mountain. His followers had turned away and were leaving, others stood silently, watching both the big man and their war leader. Little Weasel said, "You fought well."

Cougar Woman did not respond, just nodded, then turned away to return to her family and friends. As she came beside her father, he extended his arm and folded her into his chest. Her mother touched her on the shoulder and said, "We will eat soon. Have your friends join us." Cougar Woman stepped back and looked at her mother, then at her father, who nodded, and said, "I will."

19 / JOINED

Gabe led the way, trailing two horses, one with a pack, as they walked to the camp of the *Tukkutikka* and the lodge of Cougar Woman's mother and father, Pretty Cloud and Two Horses. As they neared, Gabe saw the two women busy at the cook fire, Two Horses reclined on a willow back rest and working on an arrow shaft. Cougar Woman looked up, eyes flared and without averting her eyes she spoke to her father. He lifted his head, saw the party approaching and slowly stood. Cougar Woman and her mother dropped their eyes to their work until Dove came near to join them. The women spoke with one another, Dove's excitement so evident she couldn't stand still and sat the cradle board down, leaning it against the ponderosa that shaded the camp.

Two Horses greeted Gabe with an "A-ho!" as he nodded his head. Gabe addressed him in the tongue of the Shoshone, "Greetings grandfather," using the term of great respect among the people. "I have come with gifts for you." He handed the lead ropes to Ezra and went to the pack to retrieve a blanket. He stepped before the man, spread the blanket before him, and returned to the pack. When he finished, he had arrayed a flintlock rifle and accouterments, a brass pot, two knives, a tomahawk, an assortment of packages of beads, some needles, some verdigris, and vermilion, and two folded blankets. He stepped back, took the lead lines of the two horses from Ezra and handed them to the older man.

Two Horses looked at the horses, walked close and inspected them. They were mounts taken from the Hidatsa but were good animals. One was a flashy black and white paint, the other a well-built palomino, both geldings. Two Horses was pleased with the horses, then dropped the leads to ground tie them as he went to the blanket to examine the wealth of items displayed. It was more than anyone would expect from a trader coming into the camp and trading for many pelts and more, and yet it was here, offered to him and his woman. He glanced at the items, bent to pick up the rifle, then looked to his wife, "Woman, come see," he instructed as he began to handle the rifle.

Pretty Cloud's eyes grew large as she lifted the copper pot, turning it over and moving her hands over the outside and the inside of the vessel. Then she sat down on the blanket and picked up the packages of beads, examining each one, then the needles and the packets of verdigris and vermillion. What was arrayed before her was a treasure of choice and rare items and she could hardly contain her glee. Two Horses sat down near his woman, reached for the knives and tomahawk, giving one of the knives to his woman, and hefting the others. He looked at the many items, then looked at Gabe, who had seated himself beside Ezra as they watched the couple examine the goods.

"What is this," waving his hand toward the goods and the horses, "about?" asked Two Horses.

"I would have Cougar Woman as my wife," answered Gabe.

Two Horses and Pretty Cloud looked toward Cougar Woman who was busy with Grey Dove, both trying to appear uninterested. Two Horses looked back at Gabe, "Why her?"

"She is a woman to walk beside a man. We," motioning to Ezra and himself, "explore many lands, meet many people, and that is hard for a woman. She must be strong and loyal. I believe Cougar Woman to be the match for me."

"Have you spoken with her about this?" asked Two Horses.

"We have spoken of this, yes."

Two Horses looked at his daughter, motioned her to come close and when she knelt at his side he asked her, "Do you want to go with this man?"

With her eyes down, her hands folded at her lap, she nodded and said quietly, "Yes, my father. I have never known a man that I would want as a mate until I met this man. We are to be together; I believe this."

"But you are the war leader of our people. You would leave our people without a war leader?"

"Little Weasel would have his choice of many good warriors. Our people would not be without a war leader."

"But you just fought Little Mountain who wanted to take that from you, and now you give it away?" asked her father, a little uncertain about this change of events.

"I fought him for the honor of our family, and because he would not be a good war leader. Many of our warriors would die if he was the leader. But there are many others that have proven themselves and would be a good leader."

Two Horses looked to Pretty Cloud and in that unspoken communication between couples, he had his answer. He looked at Gabe, slowly nodded his head, and said, "She is yours."

Gabe stood, extended his hand to Two Horses, who stood, and the men clasped forearms to make the pact final. The men had scarcely dropped their hands and Cougar Woman jumped into Gabe's arms, wrapped her arms around his neck and the two embraced, unashamedly, before the others. When they separated, Ezra shook Gabe's hand, and Dove hugged Cougar as she said, "You are my sister!"

***

Two Horses, Cougar Woman and Gabe went together to see Little Weasel, the chief of the band of the *Tukkutikka*. The shaman sat beside the chief as the three entered his lodge. With a wave of his hand, Little Weasel motioned them to be seated before him, but beyond the fire ring that now sat empty, save a few smoldering coals and some twigs at the edge. The shaman lifted a carved soapstone pipe, used a lighted twig to light the tobacco, took a long draught and handed the pipe to the chief. Little Weasel lifted the pipe to the four directions, upwards toward the sky and down to the earth, then took a long draught and passed the pipe to Two Horses. The motions were repeated as the pipe passed around the circle, the shaman the last to smoke. When the pipe was laid down, Little Weasel looked at Two Horses, and asked, "You wanted to speak, do so."

"Little Weasel, Big Badger," began Two Horses, addressing the chief and the shaman, "Cougar Woman has been our war leader and has led with honor, but now I speak for her, not as a war leader, but as my daughter. I have given her to this man, Spirit Bear, to be his woman, and they will leave our village to travel into the far north country."

Little Weasel looked from Two Horses to Cougar Woman, ignoring Gabe, then asked Cougar, "You would leave your people that you have led for this man?" showing a touch of incredulity and disdain for the white man that sat before them.

"This man is a great warrior. When we scouted for our village before the encampment, he fought the Blackfoot and killed many and sent the others away. He fought the Hidatsa, killed many, and returned the captives to the village of the *Agaideka* under *Owitze,* Twisted Hand. He has been a part of the *Kuccuntikka* together with his brother, Black Buffalo and his woman, Grey Dove. He will be my man and we will be together."

The chief looked at Gabe, "I have heard of this Spirit Bear, and that he is a great warrior."

He looked at Cougar Woman, "You have been a great warrior and leader of our people. Perhaps you will return someday."

"It is my wish that we will return," answered Cougar Woman.

"Then go with honor," concluded the chief, ending the audience.

***

With the camp breaking up to start the journey home, the joining ceremony was simple and quickly done. Big Badger, the shaman of the village, stood beside Two Horses and Pretty Cloud and faced the couple. Cougar Woman was outfitted in a beautiful white

tanned and intricately beaded dress, tufted fringe
hanging elegantly. Gabe thought she was beautiful and
couldn't stop smiling as she stepped beside him. Dove
had made certain that Gabe was properly outfitted
as well and had garnered a new beaded and fringed
buckskin tunic. The *boha grande* or shaman stepped
forward, gave his most intimidating stare from under
his buffalo skull cap with both horns that had small
metal bells dangling, and spoke to the couple.

"Your father has given you to this man. You will
be his woman and do as he says." He reached forward
with his knife and hacked a lock of hair from the end
of a braid, turned to Gabe and took a similar lock. He
handed the hair to Pretty Cloud which she accepted
and started braiding the locks together. Big Badger
stepped back, reached for their hands and placed
Cougar Woman's hand on Gabe's, then said, "You
are now joined. If you no longer want to be joined,
you must find this," he reached for the braid of hair,
"before you can be no longer together." Both Gabe
and Cougar knew the braid would be hidden by the
shaman, and it would not be easily found, if ever. But
they were not concerned with the lock of hair, only
with being together.

The custom of the people was for the newlywed
couple to retreat to a new lodge, set apart and in the
woods from the village, and spend their first days
in seclusion. But both villages were leaving the en-

campment to return to their summer camps. The two couples had already talked about continuing north to explore the north country and began readying their gear for the trip. They would cache the lodge in the trees near where they camped, and make whatever shelters were needed as they traveled. To carry the heavy buffalo hide lodge, even on a travois, would be too cumbersome for their journey, preferring to travel as light as possible and leave little sign of their passing. But for this night, they would use the lodge, and depart early on the morrow.

They had said their goodbyes to family and friends and watched the long lines of villagers take to the trails to return to their summer homes. As the two couples sat around the campfire, Gabe and Cougar Woman sat close, closer than usual and Dove and Ezra laughed at their giddiness. "If I didn't know better, I'd think you two were young'uns that thought you were the only two that were in love!" observed Ezra.

Both Gabe and Cougar Woman smiled, laughed, and Gabe said, "We're gonna roll our blankets out here under the stars so we can get us an early start in the mornin'."

Ezra laughed, looked at Dove and said, "You notice, he actually said that with a straight face and expected us to believe that!" The four friends laughed together, enjoying the special time together, but Chipmunk had grown restless in his cradle board and Dove said, "I will go inside and ready him for bed. He is hungry and must be fed."

Ezra stood to follow, "I guess you've already got your blankets?"

"Ummhmm, we do," answered Gabe.

"Alright then, see you in the mornin'," he said as he turned to the lodge. He glanced over his shoulder at the two, shook his head and ducked into the tipi to join Dove and Chipmunk.

20 / JOURNEY

With a wave of his hand, Gabe sent Wolf on point, searching the area for anything alarming or dangerous, guiding the group through the strange lands. It was a familiar group; Gabe leading aboard his big black, trailing the packhorse blue roan gelding, but now beside him rode Cougar Woman aboard her long-legged strawberry roan. Ezra was on his familiar bay, trailing the big mule and beside him rode Grey Dove, Chipmunk in his cradle board on her back, and trailing the steeldust mustang with a pack. Gabe noticed the steeldust was stepping high and carrying his head high, obviously relieved that he was not loaded down with the travois. All the animals seemed to step lightly, obviously glad to be on the trail. Cougar Woman was the only one that had any familiarity with the area, and that was limited, but she pointed them north as they left the scene of the grand encampment.

They turned west into a long meadow dotted with ponds and bogs, stayed to the edge of the black timber until at the head of the meadow, then took to a game trail that split the woods and followed a meandering creek. They crested a low saddle and dropped into a long basin that carried another creek that flowed north. They jumped a herd of elk that clattered through the trees, and some stopped and looked over their shoulders at the strange intruders, then stepped on into the black timber.

By late morning, they dropped into a marginal valley that held a larger river that flowed northwest and showed a well-used game trail through the sparse timber on the far side. They crossed over, took to the trail as Gabe let Ebony have his head and take the lead. The group stretched out single file and listened to the chuckle of the river just below them.

They had gone less than a mile when a roar of cascades told them there was white water ahead and the trail bent around a point to reveal a series of cascades that crashed down the steep granite face to tumble into a pool below. The trail rose up the side of the canyon wall and lifted the travelers high above the river, now a thin strip of blue and white far below that showed between the tall fir that lined the steep banks.

When they came to the edge of the timber, they were on a slight rise that overlooked a broad basin below. Fumaroles were boiling and geysers were spewing, thin clouds of steam rose from several points and the travelers sat spellbound at the image. When Gabe reined up, the others came alongside and Ezra mumbled, "It looks like the cauldron of hell itself!" The others nodded but didn't comment. The breeze that tickled the treetops also carried the sulfurous stench of the mud pots and boiling springs. The green trees before them, fir, spruce and aspen, stood in contrast to the white mineral springs and steam clouds.

Gabe stood in his stirrups, surveying the land before them and pointed to the east edge of the basin, "I think we'll stay in the trees on that side, maybe the trees'll filter some o' that stink!"

"Then let's get a move on. We're downwind of that stench now!" suggested Ezra.

Wolf was now beside Ebony, uncertain of the strange doings of the geysers and more, and Gabe spoke to him, keeping him close. Several game trails crisscrossed the woods on the east and they pushed past the 'devil's cauldron' as Ezra called it, snatching a peek through the trees as they passed. In several places, the skeletal trunks of tall spruce stood as a warning that nothing could live in the lime and silicate pools by the geysers, but Gabe pushed on through the trees, having visually marked a point that promised green grass and clear air. Although it was only about four miles from their first observation point, it seemed much farther, and although clear spring fed pools lay in the valley bottom, the ground throughout the trees still showed the white mineral from the mud pots and geysers, prompting them to keep on the move.

By early afternoon, they were at the upper end of a long green valley that showed two crystalline lakes with plenty of greenery around, which suggested good water and good graze. Gabe waved the others to the tree line while he and Wolf went to the little feeder creek that emptied into the larger of the lakes. He stepped down, looking at the banks for any mineral deposits, saw nothing but clear water, stuck his finger in it to see if it was hot water like so much of the other in this area, and was pleased to feel the coolness of a mountain spring. He scooped up a handful, took a taste and then a deep drink, satisfied it was good water. Wolf and Ebony dropped their noses into the water and sated their thirst, just as the others came near for their share.

"This is a good place to give the horses a rest, ya think?" suggested Gabe, looking at Ezra.

"Suits me!" answered Ezra, then both men felt the ground tremble beneath them, and a roar come from around the point of the ridge that followed the trail. They looked at the slope, saw steam rising beyond, and Gabe shook his head, "This is the wildest country I've ever seen! Everywhere you look there's geysers and such, and the smell! Oooeee!"

"Gives me the heebyjeebs!" declared Ezra. "Ya think we'll be out of it come night?"

"I'm hopin' so. That roarin'," nodding to the source of steam plumes, "and the ground shakin', sure don't make for good sleepin'!"

After a brief rest, giving the horses a chance to graze and taking some pemmican for themselves, they pushed on and rounded the point. All the horses were skittish, sidestepping and even Wolf stayed to the left of Ebony, his head down and picking his steps carefully. Gabe stepped down, and suggested the others do the same. He moved to the head of his horse, spoke softly to him, stroking his neck, then walked beside him, staying between his horse and the long slope of white and grey mountain with plumes of steam and a continual deep roar, acting as if it was about to explode. The blue roan stayed on the downhill side of the black, setting the example for the others and their pack animals.

No sooner had Gabe gone to ground, than they came to a steaming stream that was the outlet from the mountain. It was just a couple feet wide, and Gabe gave it a good once-over, then jumped across, pulled the reins taut and Ebony followed and the roan. With them on the far side, the others followed suit and were soon bunched together in a thick stand of trees at the base of the white slope. Although the face of the steamy mountain was only about three hundred yards wide, it was a struggle every step of the way. But once past the last of the white-faced hillside, Gabe motioned to the others and they all mounted up to move past the roaring mountain.

For another couple hundred yards, the valley bottom showed splotches of white, but it soon showed green grass and black timber, a welcome sight for the travelers. The narrow valley offered a better trail at the edge of the trees and they were able to travel two abreast, making everyone a little more comfortable to be beside one another. Gabe asked Cougar, "Have you been through here before?"

"I have not been this way, but my father told me of this place. If this is the right valley, there is a place at the end where there are cliffs that have black flint that is good for arrows."

Gabe looked at Cougar, "Then maybe we should gather up some. We won't need to make the points here, but it would be good to have the flint. It would also be good as a trade item."

Cougar Woman nodded, "It is black and makes very sharp points. My father used it to make a war axe too."

"Did he tell you how far it would be before we get out of this *land of many smokes?*"

She smiled at his expression, obviously one of dislike for the tumultuous land. "If we camp at the cliffs, it will be another day before we are free of this place. We will pass the place where we recovered the girls taken by the Hidatsa."

"So, this trail takes us to the Yellowstone River?"

"Yes, but we will pass a place different than any other. A place with many pots, different colors, and waters. You will see."

***

As they neared the end of the valley, Gabe looked at the sun, held his hand out at arm's length and calculated there to be just less than an hour before the sun set. With dusk offering diminished light, he guessed he would have about an hour to two hours to explore the cliffs and hopefully secure some flint. They stopped beside a point of trees that held some tall spruce and fir, and Gabe motioned to the others to stop and make camp. When he stepped down, Gabe bent backwards to stretch his back, then took the reins of Cougar's roan. "I'll take 'em to water, stake 'em out and let 'em get some graze. If you want, you can help Dove set up camp and such."

Cougar Woman smiled at her man, stepped forward and kissed him, an action that she had not been familiar with but had quickly learned and enjoyed. She stepped back, "Yes, my husband. I will do as you say," she ducked her head and looked up at him, smiling mischievously.

"You better! I might have to turn you over my knee and give you a good spanking!" he answered, trying to appear gruff and mean.

She laughed, mocking him as she twisted around and swatted her own bottom, and trotted off to join Dove, laughing as she left.

Gabe shook his head, laughing and started toward the small creek with the horses. Ezra had watched the antics of the two and said, "I would like to see you try to give her a spanking! She'd probably do to you like she did Little Mountain!"

***

The pillared cliffs rose straight up from the slight shoulder at the valley's edge. A dull grey, the rock cliffs held a thin cluster of fir at the top that appeared like wisps of hair standing atop the long ridge. The face of the cliff showed row after row of angular pillars, all showing rugged fissures and standing in two rows, one atop the other. At the base of the cliffs, piles of rubble and broken stone lay, and it was to this rubble that Gabe and Ezra walked. As they neared, Gabe frowned, then bent down to pick up a stone, wiped off the broken face and looked to Ezra, "This is obsidian!"

Ezra stepped close, looking at the stone in Gabe's hand. The smooth glassy surface shone black and shiny. He touched it, felt its smoothness, then touched the edge and drew back, looked at his finger and up at Gabe. "That's like glass!" he declared.

"It's from ancient lava flows and cools just like

glass. It will make fine arrow points and more." He looked down at the rubble, "But, we need to find pieces that don't show any cracks or fault lines, at least giving big enough pieces to use for what we want."

The men began scrounging, moved closer to the cliff face and looked at the pieces nearer the tall pillars and found several that they thought would be suitable. Within an hour, they had all they could easily carry and started back to camp. When they neared the fire, the women saw them walking with arms full of stone and they frowned then realized what they had and met up with them to help with the stone. As they dropped their bounty, the women marveled at the black stone, touching each piece, picking it up and looking more closely.

"Have you made points from flint before?" asked Cougar Woman.

Gabe grinned, "Yes, I learned from an Arapaho warrior. He was an excellent flint knapper and showed me some of his ways."

"Then they will be good to have with your arrows," stated Cougar Woman. She knew the arrows in Gabe's quiver were all black, made so with ashes and berries to give the look that Gabe wanted to make his arrows, when found, even more intimidating. And as he thought of the use of the obsidian, he knew she was right, and he was anxious to get started. But, this was not the time, and by having the stone with them, he could work it at his leisure.

21 / VISITORS

At first light, they were on the trail through the shadow darkened gorge away from the obsidian cliffs. In just over a mile, the canyon opened to a wide green valley, the shadows from the rising sun stretching across the flat but the wide dell beckoned with its absence of mud pots and geysers and offered a semblance of the usual pristine valleys of the high country. The creek widened and twisted its way, snakelike, through the green grass flats and the occasional cattail infested bogs. As the low timber covered hills on the west dropped away, a wider valley, about four miles across spread its breadth from mountain to mountain. The broad expanse held a herd of buffalo, probably five or six hundred head, and in the distance a herd of elk grazed. The grass was belly deep on the animals, even though the massive herd trampled it as they grazed, the remaining tall grasses, bent and partially eaten, slowly rose erect as the big beasts passed.

By midday, Gabe took a trail that split two smaller peaks and crested a small saddle before dropping into what Gabe first thought was a wasteland. The trail crossed a wide patch of grey and white rock that appeared to be the remnant of a long avalanche or rockslide, burying many trees, leaving others struggling to rise from the rubble. Then at a fork in the trail, he chose the one that pointed to a pool of blue water nestled in a cluster of fir trees. As he stood in his stirrups and shaded his eyes, it appeared that trail would take them to the canyon bottom and if Cougar Woman's memory was correct, on to the Yellowstone river. As she came alongside, he dropped into his saddle and pointed to the valley, "Is that the Yellowstone?"

She looked where he pointed, shaded her eyes, and looked back, nodding. "Yes, that is the river we followed to get the captives."

Gabe nodded, pointed to the trail that went downhill toward the blue pond, "I think that trail will be the better of the two." He nodded toward the other, "I think that'n would take us to those steam risers yonder."

They stopped at the edge of the blue pond, giving the horses a chance to graze and drink and for the riders to partake of the biscuits and strip steaks left from breakfast. The pond nestled in a little basin, with a spring fed feeder creek and a knob of a hill on the west edge.

When they started out from their mid-day break, the trail broke from the trees and overlooked a distant anomaly that immediately caught their attention. There were several small steam risers that betrayed the presence of some semblance of geyser, but the usual sulfurous stench was absent. Instead what they smelled was a sharp tinge of metal, but the steaming hot water overclouded the sensations. As they drew near, their attention was captivated by the multi-terraced hillside, with small pools of steaming water, some white, others a deep azure and crystalline clear. But the pools appeared like a conglomeration of stacked pots of stone, varying in size and color from bright white to deep umber. The formation covered almost a mile from high up the hillside to the broad base and all of a half-mile wide. While some of the pots appeared to be no higher that thin shale and randomly formed, others were pristine white with rounded edges and deeper walls. The base appeared like a smooth hump and was a dingy white, but water flowed along the sides and into the lower river beyond.

It was a marvel to see and Gabe leaned over and told Ezra, "It looks like some land-locked whale that's consuming everything in its path!"

"Yeah, but how long did it take to get this far?" asked Ezra, staring at the monolith as they rode past.

Cougar Woman had dropped back to ride beside Grey Dove and the women were silent, mesmerized at the wonder that lay before them. As they neared the far edge, Gabe reined up, frowning as he watched a tall cone, with hot water spewing from the top, and trickling down the sides. "There must be a lotta minerals in that water. See how it's forming that cone?" he asked, glancing to Ezra.

"That stuff has got to be potent!" declared Ezra, "Can you imagine what that'd do to a fella if he tried to drink it?"

"I'm purty sure if it didn't boil you as it went down, it'd kill you after you swallowed it. Course, it might take a long time, but I reckon you'd end up like some o' them statues they put up outside big city buildings!" proclaimed Gabe.

***

They followed the creek bed to the river, then took to the trail that stayed in the flats beside the river. Dusk was coming on when they came to the short canyon and the site of the Hidatsa battle, but Gabe suggested they push on through and camp at the mouth of the canyon, away from the battle site. But this was the first time seeing the scene for Dove and she stopped and looked at the grassy flat. Cougar Woman was beside her and at Dove's request, related the details of the battle. When she nodded to the rock pale at the face of the talus slope as the burial for the Hidatsa, Dove breathed deep, dropped her shoulders and gigged her buckskin forward.

The men had ridden on but waited at the far end of the small park for the women. Once reunited, they held to the trail and were soon in the open at the mouth of the canyon. They made camp at the edge of a creek that fed the Yellowstone from the west, and the men offered to try for some trout for their meal.

Ezra's way was to use a willow branch, his thin string and a hook with a grasshopper. But Gabe's way was to lay on the grassy bank and drop his hand into the water, slowly feel along the edge or under the cutaway bank, and cautiously move his hand up and grab the fish behind the gills and bring him up on the bank. Both men were successful, while Gabe brought up seven, actually eight, but Wolf took off with the first one, and Ezra six, all nice sized. They were a mix of brook and rainbow trout and one golden trout, but all would be tasty when the women finished baking them in the hot coals.

When Gabe and Ezra walked back into camp, they were surprised to see four men, warriors all, sitting near the fire and talking with the women. A frowning Gabe cautiously drew near, and recognized Shoots Running Buffalo and the three warriors that had pursued the Hidatsa, hoping to find Sacajawea. Shoots stood as Gabe and Ezra came into camp with their bounty from the creek, smiled and greeted his friends, "Ho, my friends, Spirit Bear and Black Buffalo!"

Gabe's first glance showed there was no girl with them, and he looked at Shoot's, and grinned as he spoke, "It is good to see you, Shoots Running Buffalo. Are you returning to the camp of your people?"

Shoots dropped his eyes and sat back down, he looked up at his friend, "We followed the Hidatsa for many sleeps, but they joined a big war party of Hidatsa and Crow, five hands of warriors. I think they were coming in search of the war party you fought. We could not take the captive from so many, so we came to warn others."

"Others? But everyone has left the encampment. Your people are on their way to your summer camp," explained Gabe.

Gabe handed Ezra his fish to take to the women, who were busy at the fire. Gabe seated himself on a log opposite the four men and offered, "You will eat with us?"

Shoots said, "Cougar Woman said we should eat with you. She was confident you would bring many fish for the meal," he chuckled as he looked from Gabe to Ezra as he handed off the fish. They had cut willow forks and hung the fish on the branch to carry them and both forks had considerable weight to them as Ezra handed them to the women. But the ladies went to work packing the fish in mud and raking the hot coals over the line of trout.

Shoots looked at Gabe, "Are you following the river north?"

"Well, that was the plan, but if that war party is comin' this direction, that might not be a good idea."

"There are two trails that will take you west from here." He nodded to the nearby stream, "One follows that stream, then turns to the south but goes mostly toward the setting sun. The other," and he nodded down the Yellowstone valley, "follows another stream and goes mostly west, and north some. It is over high country and is not an easy trail."

"Is not this land," started Gabe, motioning downstream of the Yellowstone, "Crow land?"

Shoots nodded, then pointed to the northwest, "Blackfoot land is there," then turning to the west and south, "Our land is there." He pointed to the northwest again, "Beyond the Blackfoot is the land of the Pend d'Oreille and Salish."

"I know about the Blackfoot, but the others, are they friendly?" asked Gabe.

Shoots grinned and answered, "Both tribes are more friendly than the Blackfoot!"

Both Gabe and Ezra laughed, then Gabe responded, "I think every tribe is friendlier than the Blackfoot! But would they allow us to pass through their land?"

"Perhaps. But no one can say any tribe will allow another to pass. It is always up to the war leader and the chief of such a tribe. If they believe you to be friendly, perhaps." Shoots looked at Gabe, and Ezra as he returned to sit beside Gabe, then suggested, "We should travel together. We will take this trail," nodding to the nearby creek, "then once across the mountains, we will join the trail of our people. We could overtake them. You could come with my people or go to the west or north from the other side of these mountains. If you continue," nodding toward the long valley of the Yellowstone, "you will meet the Hidatsa and the Crow."

"Well, that sounds like a tempting offer, Shoots, and we might just do that. But I will talk it over with Ezra and the women and then decide." He looked at the women, saw they were almost ready with the food, then suggested, "But for right now, we should eat!"

22 / FLIGHT

Shoots Running Buffalo took the lead as the party of eight left the camp at the confluence of the Yellowstone River and the small willow lined creek. The trail followed the south bank of the creek that came from the higher mountains at the headwaters about ten miles distant. They anticipated a good day of easy travel for even though the trail rose slowly to the higher elevations of the mountains, the meandering creek chuckled lazily beside them showing a mild incline to the valley.

They had taken the time for a first meal, and it was with the sun at their backs when they left the camp. The trail angled slightly toward the line of finger ridges at the upper end of the valley and moved above a pair of washed out gullies that were bottomed with thick oak brush. They were about to cross the first gulley when Wolf turned aside, went to a high knob beside the gulley and looked down their back trail. He lowered his head slightly, showed his teeth and growled, then glanced at Gabe. Gabe had watched the wolf and reined up when he took to the point, and when he looked at the back trail and growled, Gabe quickly snatched his rifle from the scabbard and the scope from the saddle bags and joined his friend on the mound.

He dropped to one knee, using the other to rest his elbow and steady the scope, adjusted the focus, and mumbled, "Oh oh, that ain't good." He looked at Wolf then to Ezra who had also stopped, motioning the others on, then called out just loud enough for his friend to hear, "I think its that Hidatsa war party. Looks like they picked up our trail. Probably following Shoots and his bunch."

He turned quickly to scan the upper end of the valley and the finger ridges that sided it, then hastily descended the little knob and said to Ezra, "Get 'em movin'! On up the valley's a better place, couple ridges that come together, good cover, if we can make it!"

Ezra dug heels to his bay and took after the others. Gabe quickly sheathed his rifle and stuffed the scope in the saddle bags as he swung aboard Ebony. Before he could do anything but lean into the wind, Ebony lunged forward, determined to overtake the bay and Ezra, and win this race. Gabe knew there was a chance the Hidatsa had not spotted them, but any good tracker would know they were not far ahead, but when they put the horses to a gallop, even the hard packed trail would turn to dust and give a sign to their pursuers that they had taken flight.

But that could not be helped, they had to get to a defensible position, and there was nothing in the valley but a few shallow gullies cut by spring runoff and snow melt, nothing good enough to fight off an overwhelming and determined enemy. He slapped legs to the big black and pushed through the dust raised by Ezra on his bay and the big mule with his packs. The blue roan pack horse tugged at the lead but was doing his best to keep pace with the black. Gabe saw Shoots and the others kick their horses to a run, although he knew they hadn't seen the Hidatsa, it was obvious they needed to put the hurry on and find cover, whatever the threat was, but, Gabe was pretty certain that Shoots would know the threat was coming from the Hidatsa and Crow.

***

Spotted Elk and Big Horn with their captive, Sacajawea, had not expected to find a war party of their own people coming toward them. Their plan was to evade the Hidatsa, maybe ally themselves with some Crow village and trade the Shoshone captive to the first French trader that offered the sought-for rifles. But they had been spotted by the war party and they could not turn away. As they came near, Spotted Elk recognized the son of their chief, Buffalo Hump. The son was known as Broken Arrow and was a respected war leader, equal in status to Spotted Elk. When Broken Arrow approached, Spotted Elk started, "It is good to see you, Broken Arrow! We are on our way to the village with this captive," motioning toward the bound Sacajawea.

"Where are the others of your party?" growled Broken Arrow, suspecting what he would hear. It would not be the first time that Spotted Elk had survived a battle and lost most of his warriors, but this was a bigger band and they were to hunt buffalo and elk, not battle with an enemy.

"The Shoshone attacked us! They were many and were like the flies on a carcass. We," motioning to Big Horn, "killed many, and escaped when they turned back and rallied for another attack. We took a hard trail over the mountains and now have found you."

"All of your warriors but you and you," nodding toward Big Horn, "are dead!" snarled Broken Arrow.

Spotted Elk hung his head, "We did what we could, but they were too many!"

Sacajawea kneed her horse forward and spat in the tongue of the Crow, "He lies! He killed one of his own and stole me and fled! There were none dead when we left!" She didn't know if the chief or anyone could understand her, but she had understood enough of what Spotted Elk said to know he was lying.

Big Horn jerked at the lead rope of the horse, pulled the animal back beside him and back handed the girl, almost knocking her off the mount. She lifted her bound hands to her split lip, wiped away the blood and glared at Big Horn.

Broken Arrow looked at Big Horn and growled, "Who lies? Spotted Elk or the girl?"

Big Horn said, "She does not know what she says!" and lifted his hand to hit her again, but Broken Arrow stopped him. He reined his horse near the girl, "Do you know who he killed to steal you?"

She nodded her head, "Yes, he was called Red Tail," she answered, lifting her head to look at Broken Arrow. "He slit his throat when he was sleeping, then took me and fled. Before that he killed my friend, White Fox. The others were following the river into the canyon, but we took the high trail into the mountains."

Broken Arrow looked at Spotted Elk who glared back defiantly, then lifted his voice and spoke to the other warriors, "This man killed one of our own, Red Tail, or so this girl says." He paused and pointed to a small group of warriors nearby, "You," including the entire group of five warriors, "will take Spotted Elk and Big Horn and this captive back to our village. The rest of us will go to the canyon to see if the others of the party are able to return with us. When we return to the village, we will go before the council to decide what will be done."

"You cannot do this!" shouted Spotted Elk and

jerked the head of his horse around to flee, but the five warriors instantly surrounded him, arrows and lances poised. Big Horn looked around as if searching for a way of escape, but Broken Arrow and another warrior pushed their horses against his and motioned for him to surrender his weapons. The others had disarmed Spotted Elk, and the leader of the group, nodded to Broken Arrow and turned to Spotted Elk, poking him in the side with his lance, motioned for Big Horn to ride beside Spotted Elk, then started them back downstream, and toward their village.

Another warrior, Takes Many Scalps, the leader of the Crow, brought his horse near Broken Arrow and asked, "What do we do now?"

"We will continue up the valley of the Yellowstone. This is the way the hunting party would return and if they are alive, we will meet them. But, if not, perhaps we will find them and then decide."

"My warriors joined with you to find some Shoshone and take some women or scalps. If we do not find some soon, we will return to our people," declared Takes Many Scalps. He was a noted warrior of his people and had earned his name and his honors. But his warriors were not here to find some lost Hidatsa, but to find captives and more. He nodded to Broken Arrow, a man several years younger, and reined his horse away. When he returned to his warriors, he explained, "We will stay one more day. If there is no promise of captives or honors, we will leave."

23 / ENCOUNTER

The head of the valley narrowed as finger ridges from both sides pushed into the slot, crowding the little stream into a cascading whitewater. The trail jammed between the rocky talus and the water, pushing aside the willows and allowing narrow passage. Shoots Running Buffalo led the way and quickly rounded the point, jerking his pony to a sliding stop and hitting the ground before the others pushed their way past.

Shoots started barking orders to his warriors, "Running Badger, Walks With a Limp, take that ridge! Black Raven, there, by the rocks at the point!" The three men ran to their appointed positions as Shoots started climbing the talus slope behind him. Cougar Woman, Ezra and Dove slid to the ground, with Cougar Woman snatching her bow and quiver and starting up the ridge. Ezra and Dove gathered the horses, moved into the trees, and hurriedly stretched out a picket line and loosely tethered all the animals.

Ezra no sooner turned around and Gabe slid the big black to a stop, snatched his rifle, bow and quiver, then on second thought pulled the two saddle pistols from the holsters at the pommel of his saddle. He dropped the weapons to the ground, trotted to the trees leading Ebony and the roan to tether them with the other animals. Within seconds he was gathering up his weapons, sat down to quickly string his bow, and as he worked, explained to Ezra, loud enough for Shoots and Cougar to hear, "It's the Hidatsa! But it doesn't look like there's as many as you said, Shoots. Maybe the others are circlin' around, but I don't think so, looks like some have left or went somewhere else, maybe up the canyon to see about the others." As he stood, he looked to Ezra, "Where's the others?"

Ezra quickly filled him in on the positions of the other warriors, then asked, "So, where d'ya want me'n Dove, captain?"

Gabe frowned, "Captain?"

"Well, I'm used to takin' orders from you whenever we get in a fix like this, so . . ." he grinned as he stood with his war club hanging on his back and his Lancaster rifle in his hands. His over/under double barreled pistol protruded from his belt beside his tomahawk. Gabe glanced at Dove as she stood with her rifle in hand and possibles pouch and powder horn hanging over her shoulder. Gabe glanced around, "How 'bout here on the face of this talus slope. There's plenty of rocks for cover and you'll have a clear field of fire as they come up the draw."

Ezra nodded, turned to Dove and they started working their way up the rockpile to find a firing position. Gabe turned and started climbing the ridge, wanting high ground to see the entire valley and any approach of the Hidatsa. Once in position with Wolf at his side, he hunkered down beside a large boulder and slipped the scope from the case hanging at his side. He saw the band following their trail about five or six hundred yards distant and he focused in on the group. As he scanned the crowd, he counted and tallied fourteen, a lot less than the twenty-five or six that Shoots had reckoned were in the bunch.

He adjusted his focus and concentrated on the leaders and those near, then quickly scanned the rest. He turned to look down the ridge past Cougar Woman who was about six yards below him, to Shoots, another five or six yards toward the point of the ridge. He raised his voice and asked, "Didn't you say there were Crow with the Hidatsa?"

Shoots turned toward Gabe and answered, "Yes, two hands of Crow."

"No Crow with that bunch. Looks like they're all Hidatsa!" responded Gabe, lifting the scope again. The Hidatsa started spreading out, coming forward slowly, lances held across their thighs, bows at their sides with arrows nocked. The leader was at the front with a typical Hidatsa headdress with many feathers and in Gabe's mind, resembling a porcupine. He was covered with black and red tattoos, his long hair hanging loosely over his shoulders. The man beside him had a buffalo horn skull cap, tattooed shoulders, and a bone pipe breast plate.

Gabe gauged the distance to be about four hundred yards, paused a moment then slipped the scope back in the case and pulled his quiver close. He pulled out an arrow, stepped beside the big boulder and looked at the Hidatsa as they approached. He waited a couple moments, then lifted the bow and brought it to full draw, lifted it a bit more, angling the arrow upwards, the let it fly. Instantly the arrow whistled its screaming cry as it sailed in an arch toward the attackers. Gabe watched as the warriors showed confusion, looking upwards, shading their eyes, trying to control their skittish mounts, as the screaming arrow plunged toward them and impaled itself in the deep grass less than three yards in front of the leader. It took him and the others nearby a moment to settle their horses, then the leader barked orders to a warrior, who jumped from his mount and searched for the arrow, and moments later retrieved the screamer to hand it to his leader.

The leader examined it, handed it to the buffalo horn cap who also looked it over carefully. Then the leader looked at the ridges, lifted his lance into the air and shouted his war cry, slapping legs to his horse and starting the charge. The other warriors instantly responded with their own war cries and the attack surged forward.

Gabe had already nocked another arrow, and as the line of warriors moved together, he sent the arrow on its way, not waiting to see it strike, then another and another, each to a different point on the line of attackers. The second arrow was a perfect strike, burying itself in the chest of a warrior and carrying him to the ground to be trampled by those behind him. The third arrow also found its mark, but impaled a warrior low in his stomach and pinning him to the back of his horse, but he struggled free and fell to the side, his mount bucking and snorting trying to free his back of the broken arrow shaft. The fourth arrow whispered past the head of the leader to bury itself in the shoulder of the horse behind, causing it to stumble and throw its rider over his head, to crumple in the grass with a broken neck.

Broken Arrow saw the warriors fall, looked ahead, and knew they were still too far for their own weapons but were within range of rifles and started to rein aside when smoke blossomed from the ridge and two more warriors fell. He screamed and reined his mount aside, drawing his warriors with him as they moved toward the trees at the base of a small finger ridge. As they came to a stop, Broken Arrow looked around, counting his men and knew they had suffered too any losses. With a band of fourteen, counting himself and the shaman, Two Horns, he had already lost half of his warriors.

***

Gabe grabbed for his scope and searched the ridge and trees for the Hidatsa, but they were hidden behind the ridge. He looked down at Cougar Woman and Shoots, "How 'bout we get outta here 'fore they decide to charge again! I think we have time to make some tracks 'fore they work up the courage."

Shoots looked at the narrow valley before him, the finger ridges and timber and saw only the fallen warriors. He looked up at Gabe, "Yes, we will go!" and rose to signal his men. Within moments, the entire group was moving at a canter up the trail that would take them deeper into the mountains and offering greater cover and protection from a frontal attack like just happened. Gabe hung back, repeatedly finding a promontory to check their back trail and saw no evidence of anyone following, but it wasn't until just after mid-day that he was satisfied the Hidatsa had ended their pursuit.

***

Broken Arrow looked at Two Horns, then lifted the black whistling arrow that lay across the withers of his horse, "This," shaking the black shaft, "was a warning! We should have heeded and stopped or turned back! No man can shoot an arrow as far as that," nodding toward the flats of the meadow where his warriors lay, "and take down our warriors."

"It is an omen!" declared the shaman. "They are evil spirits, aaiiieee!" he screamed as he lifted a gourd rattle overhead, shaking it as if to ward off the spirits. "We must leave this place!" he declared, "I have seen it!" He shook his head, lifting the gourd high and shaking it as he moaned a chant.

Broken Arrow looked at the meadow, saw movement and then the figure of one of his men, stood, stumbling, and staggering toward them. He was reminded of the times when Spotted Elk had led war parties and had he been leading this one, he would have been angered and determined to charge the enemy, regardless the cost to his own warriors. But Broken Arrow was not Spotted Elk, he considered the loss of his warriors and the cost of continuing this fight. This was not worth the loss of another warrior. He looked around, saw another warrior sit up, but he moved no further, yet he looked toward the huddled group that sat their horses beside the trees. Broken Arrow looked around, motioned for the others to remain, and reined his mount toward the downed warrior. He walked his horse through the tall grass, glancing from his warriors to the ridge, fearing the sound of another whistling arrow, but none came. He reached down and helped his warrior up behind him, then rode to each of the others to see if any still lived. One other, the last to fall, was lying in the grass, holding his side where blood had pooled on his belly, and looked up at his leader. Broken Arrow motioned to the band for another to come get this man, then started for the trees with his wounded warrior behind him.

Three were dead, three were wounded, and as Broken Arrow looked at his men, he knew they were outraged but also fearful after their shaman had spoken. He dropped to the ground, lifted the wounded man down and directed the others to tend to the wounded. "When they can travel, we will leave this place. Our shaman says it is an evil place, and this," motioning to the three wounded men now propped against the trees, "shows he is right. We must leave!" he declared, allowing no argument.

Because he was able to retrieve his wounded, Broken Arrow was certain the ones they sought were gone and there was no reason to follow, only to have more casualties. By early afternoon, the dead were retrieved, the wounded cared for, and the entire band mounted up and started from this valley of death. When they came to the mouth of the canyon of the Yellowstone, he sent two warriors into the canyon to see if there was any sign of the other band that had been abandoned by Spotted Elk.

The two warriors that went into the canyon overtook the band beside the Yellowstone and well downriver. When they reported their find of the burial, the leader and others wailed the deaths of their friends but were relieved *they* were alive and would soon return to their village and their families.

24 / SEPARATION

At the head of the valley, both the stream and the trail forked at the point of a hogback ridge. Shoots led the way to the right fork that took them into a shallow valley that lay between two mountains. The one on the south showing black timber and the one on the north bald slopes with spotty timber and mostly scrub oak, with big granite shoulders that marked several draws formed by eons of snow melt and avalanches of deep glacier deposits. Before them, the trail climbed toward two fan shaped rim rock slopes, but the trail soon took them through the thick woods as it climbed, zig zag, at the side of the fan like ridges.

They crossed over the timbered saddle and stopped near the crest. Shoots stepped down and stretched, prompting the others to follow suit. It was never an easy trek riding uphill on such a steep trail, where the riders worked almost as hard as the horses, shifting weight, ducking branches, prompting the mounts onward and upward. But now, both riders and horses had a breather.

Cougar Woman stood beside Gabe as they gazed at the magnificent panorama. Before them and beyond, mountain after craggy granite tipped mountain raised their hoary heads for recognition. There were sky scratching peaks that held glaciers and snowpack in their crevices, flat topped buttes that stood as tables for the gods, ridges, rimrock, valleys, canyons, and more. As Gabe's eyes touched each point, he wondered if man ever set foot on that place. Although he knew the native peoples had roamed the wilderness, with such a vast land, surely there were places that no man had ever seen or walked upon.

Shoots stepped near, lifted his hand and pointed to a cut in the mountains before them, "We will go through there. Our village will be in that great flat beyond. Two sleeps, we will be there. My woman, Laughing Antelope, waits for me."

Gabe looked where he pointed, knew that was the land where he had fought Moon Walker, the man who had killed his wife, Pale Otter, a land of sad memories. He looked at Shoots, nodded to the west, "And there?"

"It is the land of our winter camp, and there," pointing north of the distant range, "is the land of the Pend d'Oreille, Salish, and beyond to the land of the Nez Perce." He paused, turned to look at his friend, Spirit Bear, and asked, "You would go there?"

"Perhaps."

Shoots pointed to a far valley, "There is the Red Rock River, while it flows toward the setting sun, it is the land of the *Agaideka* Shoshone, but when it flows north, it goes into the land of the Blackfoot. Beyond that is the Salmon river, our people go there to trap Salmon to smoke for winter. It flows north, but when it turns to the west, it goes into the land of the Nez Perce, but north of that bend is the land of the Pend d'Oreille and Salish."

"Then we will stay in the land of the *Agaideka.* There is much to see here," stated Gabe, but he knew deep within that they would not limit their explorations and discoveries to the land of their Shoshone brothers.

They dropped off the saddle and took a little used game trail that shouldered the long ridge and took them to the north. They made camp in a small basin beside a small teardrop shaped lake that lay at the head of a long valley that Shoots said would take them to the parting of their ways. It would be at the bottom of this valley where Shoots and his warriors would go north to their village, but Gabe and company were bound to the western lands.

They made camp, and Shoots had his men spell one another so at least one stood guard throughout the night. Gabe and company were less concerned as he had taken a long look-see at their back trail while they stopped on the saddle and saw nothing but the usual wildlife, none of which were spooked at strange passersby. With the horses and Wolf always vigilant, the two couples slept well, and as usual, Gabe and Ezra were the first to rise, each having chosen a place for their morning time with the Lord. They went to their places by the fading light of the moon and the stars, and soon returned to camp.

Shoots and his men had already packed their gear and stood by their horses as Gabe and Ezra returned. Shoots stepped forward, extended his arm, "We are anxious to be home and will leave now. You have been a good friend and warrior for my people, we are grateful. You," he paused, looked at the others, "all of you, will always be welcome in our village and by our fires." Shoots reached for Gabe's arm and the two clasped forearms, adding their free hand to the clasp and stepping close.

Gabe said, "You have been a good friend also, Shoots, and you and yours will always be welcome at our fires as well. Go in peace and speak to your wife and your people for us."

"I will," answered Shoots, then stepped before Ezra to clasp his forearm and say his good bye. The men swung aboard and left the camp, none looking back.

Gabe sat beside the fire, elbows on his knees, as he watched them leave, then turned to Cougar Woman, "Got'ny coffee?"

She smiled, pointed to the pot and cup, letting him know he was to pour his own, and smiled and went about her work as she and Dove finished the preparation of their breakfast. Gabe poured himself a cup, poured one for Ezra and sat down. He looked at Ezra, "So, that faraway country callin' you like it is me?"

Ezra grinned as he nodded, "Ummhmmm, and from what we saw, there's a lot of it!"

"Ain't there though. I think that somewhere in the middle of all these mountains, we should be able to find us a place to light a spell, don't you?"

"I thought we did, back on the Popo Agie, but no, 'bout the time you think there's moss growin' under your feet, you wanna get up and go!" He chuckled as he thought about it then added, "I'm hopin' that Cougar Woman there slows you down some. Mebbe after you an' her get a passel o' youngun's runnin' around, you might try to land somewhere for a spell."

Gabe leaned back, locked his fingers behind his head, and glanced at Ezra, "Now you know it ain't my fault that every time we think we're settled, some hombre raises his ugly head and causes us or somebody else problems and we get drawn right in the middle of it."

Ezra shook his head, "Well, you don't have to go lookin' for it all the time!"

The good-natured bantering was common with the two life-long friends, and the women watched and listened, prompting Dove to explain to Cougar Woman that their conversation was quite common for them and had oft been repeated. But their repartee was stopped when Dove called, "Time to eat!"

***

"You are right!" declared an exhausted Snake Eater. He dropped to the ground beside Little Mountain, "I trailed them north, but they joined with some *Agaide-ka,* and went west. If we keep to the valley of this river, we should overtake them soon!" Snake Eater's shoulders drooped before he leaned back against the log where Little Mountain sat, his makeshift crutch lying beside him.

"It is good! We will hit them and take Cougar Woman. She will be my woman, or I will kill her!" snarled the vengeful Little Mountain. He had wanted Cougar Woman for as long as he could remember but she always shunned him, angering him more each time. Then she humiliated him before the villagers when they fought. He should have never held back, but he did not want to kill her, just put her in her place so he could become the war leader. He never expected her to fight so hard and she moved like the catamount she was named after. He could not hold her, and she fought him so viciously, but now he would have his revenge.

He had continued to recruit followers, even after Lean Bear had been chosen as war leader. There were always those on the fringe that would follow anyone that promised honors or vengeance, even though they had not been wronged. And when Little Mountain said, "Cougar Woman has been taken by the white man! She did not want him, she wanted me, but he paid a great price and her father wanted the rifle for his own. Now we must find her, kill the white man and his friend, and bring her back to her people!"

Several had listened to his rant, most did not believe him, and left. But the few that did had been his followers for some time. Crooked Tree, Rams Horn, and Bent Nose had long been faithful followers of Little Mountain for it was easier to follow him than fight him, as is the way with bullies and their followers. Snake Eater had been his friend since they were children and he still followed the big man.

After his fight with Cougar Woman, Little Mountain spent little time licking his wounds and more time trying to convince Little Weasel, the chief, that he should be war leader. But the council had turned him away and chosen Lean Bear, which angered Little Mountain and convinced him the only way he could be vindicated, was to find and return Cougar Woman to the people, proving he was the better man and worthy of being war leader.

While he formed his plan, he also had a woman tend his wounds and bind his leg. With his forked branch crutch, he was able to move about and work his plan. When Cougar Woman and the white man left the village, he sent Snake Eater after them, then gathered the others to start their pursuit, believing he knew where they were going and could intercept them. He had questioned Two Horses about the white man and what he would do, but Two Horses said all he knew was they were going to the north country, prompting Little Mountain to take to the easternmost fork of the three rivers, the river that would one day be known as the Gallatin, but now was only known as the east fork.

When Gabe and company had taken the trail that led them to the Yellowstone, Little Mountain went west to the headwaters of the east fork and followed that north. Now, according to Snake Eater, they were within a day, maybe two, of where they would find Cougar Woman. Little Mountain grinned at the thought, his lip curling in a snarl as his eyes squinted, thinking about what he would do to the woman that had humiliated him before his own people. He would have his vengeance soon.

25 / RESPITE

When the men finished their second cup of coffee, Gabe looked at Ezra and asked, "Are we in a hurry to get somewhere?"

Ezra leaned back, frowning, and replied, "Uh, not that I know of, why?"

"I was thinkin' 'bout stayin' here a day or two. We need to clean our weapons and such, and I was thinkin' about givin' that spare rifle to Cougar Woman and takin' the time to show her how to use it."

Ezra let a slow smile cross his face, "That sounds fine to me." He looked around the camp, then to the distant peaks, "This is a comfortable camp, we could stay here a good long while if you want," he drawled, reaching for the coffee pot to pour himself another cup.

Gabe brought out the rifle, a Lancaster similar to Ezra's, with the name *William Henry* engraved on the side of the barrel opposite the lock. At .48 caliber, it was a smidge lighter than Ezra's and the barrel about two inches shorter. Gabe had a pouch full of balls and patches for the rifle and dropped it into his spare possibles pouch. With the pouch, powder horn, and rifle in hand he walked to Cougar Woman who had just seated herself beside the large flat boulder they had used for a prep table and lay the weapon and accouterments beside her. Cougar glanced at the rifle then up at Gabe with a bit of a frown and asked, "What?"

Gabe smiled, "That's your new rifle!" he declared.

"Mine?" she asked, then looked back at the rifle. She stood up, reached for the weapon and lifted it to her shoulder like she had seen Gabe do, then looked at Gabe and asked, "Why? I have my bow and lance."

"Yeah, but it might be useful for you to have your own rifle and add to the firepower of our little band. I figgered we'd walk out there," nodding toward the clearing at the foot of the long ridge, "and give it a try. Want to?"

Cougar Woman lifted her eyebrows, pursed her lips, and looked at Gabe with a bland expression, and said, "If Dove comes with us, yes." The women looked at one another, both understanding that what they were doing with rifles was more for the men than for themselves. Dove went to their stacked gear and retrieved her rifle and pouch, then walked beside Cougar Woman as they followed the men to the clearing.

With the preliminaries, loading, priming and more, out of the way, Gabe picked up a big piece of ponderosa bark and walked into the clearing, propped it up and walked back. He looked at Dove, "How 'bout you showing her how it's done," he suggested. Dove smiled, primed her rifle, then with a glance to Cougar, lifted it to her shoulder and took aim. She brought the hammer to full cock, setting the triggers, then with a narrowed aim, she squeezed off her shot. The puff of dust from the bark told of a good hit, and Dove smiled at the praise given by Ezra and Gabe.

Gabe stepped beside Cougar and talked her through the steps, reminded her about setting the triggers, then stepped back. Cougar was as still as her namesake as she lined up the front blade with the buckhorn sight at the rear of the barrel, then slowly squeezed off her shot. The long rifle bucked, spat smoke from the frizzen pan and the barrel, rocked Cougar back on her heels, and spat lead at the target. The big ball found its mark and split the bark. Gabe reached his arm around Cougar's shoulders and hugged her close, "You're a natural!" he declared, smiling.

Cougar eagerly reloaded and primed her rifle, ready for another practice shot, while Ezra set the two pieces of the bark back up and returned to their side. While she worked, she said, "In the time it takes me to load this for one shot, I could launch four, five arrows, maybe more!"

Gabe chuckled, agreed with her, then added, "But, this rifle can shoot a mite further than you can send an arrow."

Cougar looked at him, "Then maybe you make me a bow like yours. It can shoot as far as this rifle!"

"You're right about that, but it took me almost this many," holding up both hands with all fingers showing, "winters before I became skilled and strong enough to use that bow. I don't think you want to spend that time, and I don't think I want you getting that strong!"

Cougar looked at him with a frown, "Why you no want me to get strong?"

"Then you might whip me like you did Little Mountain!" declared Gabe, laughing.

***

When they returned to camp, Cougar was shown how to properly clean her rifle as the others cleaned theirs. Gabe had long held to the practice that only one of his weapons would be cleaned then reloaded, before starting another. He never wanted to be without a loaded weapon nearby and Ezra had the same practice. It was mid-afternoon when they finished the usual chores of cleaning weapons, repairing any tack, and sorting the items of the packs. Dove and Cougar had suggested the men go for some fresh meat while they looked for plants to add to their fare.

While the men readied their horses and the pack mule, the women rigged slings for their rifles and emptied a parfleche to use for their plants and more. Dove said, "We will follow the creek into the flat, but we will not go into the canyon."

Ezra looked at Gabe and back at his woman, "I think we're goin' that way," pointing to the north along the edge of the steep sided ridge and taller mountains. "We'll be lookin' for elk, or maybe bighorns." The couples embraced and parted to their opposite directions, the women afoot, the men mounted and leading the pack mule.

As the women left the camp, they were chattering and walking with a bounce in their step and Gabe looked at them, back to Ezra, "Guess they'll be enjoying the time alone."

"Well, we won't, that's for sure. Hunting is such hard work, don't know how anybody can enjoy themselves!" proclaimed Ezra, doing his best to maintain a straight face as he mounted his bay. Both men laughed and started their mounts away from the grassy clearing and into the trees. From their prayer promontories on the side of the mountain behind the lake, they had spotted the creek that carved its way through the black forest and made its way west to the distant river. The area was thick with aspen and fir and showed itself to be prime country for elk, and even bighorns that might come down from the high country for water in the creek. They wanted to be in place near some of the small parks beside the creek by late afternoon, pre-dusk, the time when animals came from their beds and went to water before grazing in the half-light of dusk.

With Wolf trotting before them, they followed a scant game trail that wound through the trees, slowly making its way into the wide basin and the narrow creek. As they approached the tree line before a small park, Wolf stopped, one paw lifted, head lowered, and letting a low growl come from deep within. Gabe reined up, twisted about to see what had stopped Wolf, stood in his stirrups, but saw nothing. He pulled his rifle from the scabbard and stepped down, moving up behind Wolf who still had not moved. Gabe went to one knee beside him and scanned the edge of the park, then he saw movement.

He leaned to one side, trying to see around a big fir tree, smelling it before he saw it, and looked at a big brown grizzly, pawing at a long dead tree trunk, probably looking for grubs. Behind the grizz were two smaller duplicate images, cubs, who were learning about what mom was trying to teach them, and both clawed at the rotten wood. As the big bear moved, she grunted and grumbled, digging into the deep orange of the rotten wood and occasionally stopping to devour her treasures. Suddenly she jerked her head around and stared in the direction of Gabe and company. She lifted to her hind legs, let out a roar that vibrated the trees and penetrated Gabe's being with a touch of fear. She was a monster and had apparently gotten a whiff of their smell. The eyesight of a grizzly is not the best, but they make up for it with their sense of smell and awareness of their environment. She pawed the air, growled again with her lower jaw dropping and her mouth showing big enough to swallow Gabe's head whole if she got her teeth into him.

Ezra was now beside him, rifle in hand, and whispered, "I think we better high-tail it 'fore she decides we're the grubs she's huntin'!"

Gabe answered by slowly standing, touched the back of Wolf and backstepped to Ebony, who was standing, ears forward, nostrils flaring, and looking through the trees. He might not have seen the bear, but he certainly heard it and obviously didn't like what he heard, and the smell of bear was in the air. Gabe swung aboard, kept his rifle across his thighs and reined a very willing Ebony around and started through the trees, Wolf again leading the way. With many glances over his shoulder, Gabe gigged Ebony to a faster pace, but the big black was already moving as fast as the thick timber allowed. Within a few moments, they had put a rocky mound between them and the bear and turned back to the north to make their way to a lower part of the creek.

***

The women had gone but a short ways when Cougar Woman had grown tired of the weight of the rifle at her back. "You wait. I will leave this at camp and get my bow and quiver," she declared, and trotted away, intent on retrieving a weapon she was both skilled with and comfortable with, and a lot easier to carry while they were scrounging for plants. As she left, Dove spotted a familiar bush and went to it, the ripe red berries begging to be picked, and she began plucking the ripe currant berries and dropping them into the parfleche. Cougar Woman returned, spotted her friend, and joined her in the harvest.

Within a short distance they found raspberries, strawberries, and some elderberries. And a short ways further, some huckleberries and chokecherries to add to the batch. A rocky escarpment yielded some biscuitroot, and the edge of a clearing beside the stream offered an abundance of camas bulbs. Cougar Woman also spotted some late budding aspen and plucked the red buds to make a salve. With their last find of osha and yampa, the women were pleased with their harvest and started back to camp.

But within a few steps, Cougar whispered, "Stop," and dropped to one knee. She nodded to the trees at the side of the little clearing and they watched as shadows seemed to move. They dropped the parfleche as Dove slipped her rifle from her back, primed it, and stood ready. Cougar had nocked an arrow, watching the movement, and waited. Suddenly two little shadows scampered up a tree and the bigger one lifted up to watch her youngsters shinny out on a large branch of the towering spruce. The momma black bear was only concerned about her playful cubs, watched as they stopped and looked down, then with a growl of warning, she bent her head around to look toward the two women.

Both women smiled at the antics of the black bear family, and slowly and cautiously picked up the parfleche, each one gripping the loop of rope and started through the trees and back to camp. With several glances over their shoulders to ensure they weren't followed, they laughed together and walked, chattering all the way, back to the camp.

***

Gabe had yielded the lead to Ezra and took the lead of the mule from him, letting him pass by and choose the path through the close aspen. The leaves overhead fluttered, flashing green and white, as the hunters passed, waving them on as they twisted and turned through the white barked trees. A small park showed through the trees, with the darker pines beyond and the willows and alders beside the creek. Ezra reined up and stood in his stirrups for a better look, then dropped in his seat and twisted around to look at Gabe. He spoke softly, "This looks good with the aspen yonder that follow that draw up the ridge, and it looks like there's another meadow below this'n. Mebbe one of us could stay here and the other'n go to the next one."

"Sound good to me. It's gettin' 'bout time for some of 'em to be comin' from the trees and goin' for water. So, you stay here an' I'll take the next park."

Ezra nodded and swung his leg over the rump of his bay. He loosened the girth as Gabe passed him by, and said, "Good luck!'

"And to you as well," answered Gabe, tugging on the lead line of the mule. He looked down at Wolf at his side, "Wolf, stay with Ezra." The big wolf looked up at Gabe, moved to the side and sat down to let him pass, then looked at Ezra with an expression that said, "Well, come on."

Gabe moved across the little meadow, tethered the horse and mule on the downhill side and well into the trees. Loosened the girths, then took his bow and quiver as he went to the tree line and sat down to string the bow. Just as he finished with the bow and started to rise, he smelled elk, then he heard them. He slid behind a good-sized spruce, the smooth trunk of the big tree shielding him from view and watched as a mature cow elk tip toed into the clearing. Her head was down, her neck hung heavy with the darker brown hair that blended with her chest. The thin line of dark trailed the top of her neck and down the middle of her back. The tawny sides faded to the yellow/white of her rump. Her dark legs pushed through the grass as she scouted the meadow.

A long legged and awkward calf scampered after his mother, leading the way for two more cows with calves and a lone cow, trailing the pack. Gabe watched as they moved through the grass, intent on the creek and the break in the willows that offered access to the water. Gabe stood unmoving, watching, waiting. He would take the sole cow that was without a calf, ensuring the other calves would not lose their mothers. The elk appeared a little skittish, perhaps they had a whiff of horse or man, or maybe it was the grizzly back in the trees uphill from them. But Gabe nocked an arrow, let them drink then move into the grass for some graze, then waited for a clear shot at the lone cow.

The animals moved slowly, but the herd cow stayed vigilant and Gabe moved only his eyes as he waited. Finally, the big old cow moved to the tree line as if readying to leave, the others lined out behind her and then the lone cow bent her head for another snatch of grass, and started to lift it to follow the others, but Gabe's arrow whispered from the trees and impaled the animal, piercing her lower chest, until only the fletching of the arrow showed. She stumbled forward a couple of steps, her head hanging, then fell on her chest and dropped. The other elk moved quickly away, not frightened, but confused, and soon disappeared in the dark timber.

Gabe watched the downed cow for movement, saw none, walked close and poked her neck with his toe but there was no reaction. He stepped back, emitted the scree of the nighthawk, knowing Ezra would hear it and know he had taken an animal. He heard the answering call and turned to go to fetch his horse and mule. They quickly field dressed the cow, leaving the gut pile for the carrion eaters, after Wolf had his fill of the innards, then loaded the mule and started back to camp.

The women were glad to see them as they came into the camp, mule loaded with elk. With everyone helping, the carcass was hung from the nearby spruce, the horses rubbed down, watered and picketed, and the men relieved the women of the task of skinning the elk and cutting it up. But the women took select portions of the back strap and prepared it for their supper. This night would be a busy one, cutting and smoking the meat, cleaning the hide, and keeping everything from the reach of varmints. But that would mean there would be more than one fire going to smoke the meat and would be tended all night. But the end product would be worth the effort.

26 / SMOKE

The sun was high overhead when Little Mountain pulled his horse to a stop. This was familiar country to the big man; they had hunted this land and had traveled through here when they raided the Nez Perce. The river they followed flowed due north then turned to the northwest and just over two miles, a massive horseshoe shaped basin lay on the right or north of the river. It was that basin that made the long ridge pointing to the northwest and ended with the tall peaks. The same long ridge that held the saddle with the trail crossing from the east, and probably the trail used by the *Agaideka* and the white man who stole Cougar Woman.

Little Mountain looked from Snake Eater to the others, "We will find their trail there," pointing to the long ridge, "and find them soon." Without waiting for any response from his followers, Little Mountain nudged his horse off the trail beside the river and led the group into the wide basin below the ridge. They followed a zig-zag course, staying at the edge of the trees that covered the west slope of the long ridge, watching for any sign of the passing of their prey. It was a difficult route, with many gulches made by snowmelt and spring floods, until Little Mountain opted for an easier passage and took to the lower flats. Although out in the open, it was easier going and his leg bothered him, every lance of pain adding to his resolve to get his revenge whether by killing the white man and taking the woman or killing them both.

By the time they mounted the hogback finger ridge that extended into the basin from the long rimrock ridge, the sun had dropped behind the western horizon and the light of dusk offered just enough light for them to make camp. Little Mountain begrudgingly made the stop, his leg causing him great pain and aggravation, but he noted they were close to the saddle crossing of the higher ridge, and nearer the trail where he expected they would find sign from the woman and the white man. As he slid to the ground, he grabbed his crutch and hobbled to a log. He looked at Snake Eater, "We will find them tomorrow! They will not be far, the crossing is there," he pointed with his stick, "and we will find their sign."

He stretched out his leg, rubbing it and checking his bandages. The woman that tended him had used a wide piece of dried raw hide, hair on and bent to the shape of his leg, to fashion a splint, then wrapped it tight with soft buckskin to keep it stable. His leg had swollen, and the binding was unyielding. In his aggravated state, he angrily undone the binding and dropped the splint to the ground, giving him immediate relief. He leaned back, stretching his leg, felt a stabbing pain and jerked himself upright as he winced and groaned. He shook his head, forced himself to breathe deep and slow, then finally relaxed enough to look around at his men, who were watching him as they prepared their camp.

Snake Eater said, "I have rolled out your blankets," nodding to the edge of the trees and the blankets under the long branches of a ponderosa. "Do you want me to help you?" he offered.

"No!" spat Little Mountain, "I can do it myself!" but when he rose, he grimaced from the pain and almost fell, caught himself and with his makeshift crutch, hobbled to his blankets. He slowly lowered himself, then stretched out. He lifted up on his elbows, looking at the men, "Bring me some pemmican!" he growled at Snake Eater, and watched as his long-time friend meekly brought him a pouch of pemmican pieces and held it out to him. Little Mountain snatched it, moaned as he lay down, then rolled to his side to eat. Snake Eater walked back to the others where a small fire had been started, sat down and put his elbows on his knees, shaking his head slightly as he stared into the flames.

Bent Nose looked at Snake Eater, "Can he ride tomorrow?"

Snake Eater glanced over his shoulder at the big man now on his blankets, back at Bent Nose and answered, "His anger will give him strength. He believes Cougar Woman was stolen, but she was not. He will not listen to anyone that says different."

"He said he wants to take her back, but I think he wants to kill her," suggested Crooked Tree. His comment elicited nods from the others until Ram's Horn said, "It is not right to kill one of our own. She fought him and shamed him, but she is not at fault."

"What are you saying?!" growled Little Mountain from the trees. He had risen to one elbow and glared at the others.

"We need fresh meat!" answered Snake Eater. "We should hunt for some!"

"Ahgh, it will be too dark. Hunt in the morning!" ordered the big man, dropping back on his blankets, flinching from the pain.

***

After Gabe and Ezra heard the women tell of the black bear and her cubs they saw while hunting plants, the men swapped tales about the grizzly they encountered. And with the bears and other usual predators they agreed to take turns watching the camp and tending the smoke fires throughout the night. Cougar took the first watch, was relieved by Dove, then Ezra, then Gabe was awakened to take the last watch. While the others snoozed, he checked the three smoke fires, stirred the coals, and put a few pieces of dried pine on the coals, then added some more alder sticks for the smoke. The elk hide had been staked out and scraped clean, but Gabe knew the smell of blood was still in the camp. Even the smoking of the meat brought the aroma of cooking meat, but added with the smoke of fire, any predators would be a little confused, but still curious.

He paced slowly around the camp, staying within the trees where possible and using the carpet of pine needles to quiet his passing. He listened to the night sounds, frogs by the edge of the small lake, the rattle of cicadas, the cry of a nighthawk on the hunt, and the occasional question of an owl. When the howl of a wolf lifted, Wolf stopped and looked in that direction. He had been at Gabe's side, but now looked from Gabe to the direction of the howl, then trotted into the trees and lifted his answering howl. Gabe stopped, listened, and grinned, knowing the big wolf that was his companion, was still as wild as if he were leading his own pack, and might go in pursuit of the lonely female that had sounded her call for a mate. Gabe lifted his shoulders in a heavy sigh, knowing he would not want to lose his friend, but also knowing the call of the wilderness was strong.

Their camp was on the west of the long ridge that rose high above their camp, and the rising sun would cast long shadows over them until just shy of mid-morning. Yet Gabe and Ezra had long had the practice of meeting with the Lord at the start of every day, and as the lanterns of the night sky began to diminish, Ezra rolled from his blankets, nodded to Gabe as the men started away from the camp to go to their separate points of rendezvous with the Lord. Gabe started to leave, then remembered to fetch his scope for his morning look-see, then with the rifle on a sling at his back, he climbed the steep slope to the top of the talus and his promontory above the rimrock. When he came to his place, he looked around for the missing Wolf and saw nothing, then took his seat on the clay dirt before the rock, leaned back and looked at the remaining stars and setting moon of the night sky. The hint of grey showed above the ridge that rose to his left, and as the dim light of early morning showed, he finished his prayers, and started to read. His chosen passage was from I Chronicles, chapter four, and finished with verse ten, *"And Jabez called on the God of Israel, saying, Oh that thou wouldest bless me indeed, and enlarge my coast, and that thine hand might be with me, and that thou wouldest keep me from evil, that it may not grieve me! And God granted him that which he requested."* He looked at it again, thought. *That should be my prayer. But is it evil when I kill to protect?* He shrugged, lay the bible aside and picked up his scope.

He scanned the valley beyond the rise, the valley they would take to the river below, then moved slowly back to the south, searching the river valley, the closer hills, and the further most point of the valley where the river emerged from the canyon. He saw a small herd of elk walking towards the river, probably for their morning water, a few deer that tiptoed through the grassy flats, then a shadow moved, and two more behind it and Gabe grinned as he recognized the black bear and her cubs that the women had seen. He brought the scope along the edge of the ridge, scanning the timber and the flats, then lowered it to search the nearer timber and clearings. He was hoping to see the grizzly moving further away but was disappointed.

Then he saw something that didn't belong, and it moved. He focused in on the object, watched, then recognized it was a paint horse, and as he looked through the thin aspen grove, he saw other horses, and they were tethered so they weren't wild horses. He breathed easy, watching, searching, and then a thin wisp of smoke lifted straight up from the trees, then was gone. But he knew he was not mistaken, it was smoke. They had visitors.

There was other movement, but in the dim light of early morning, he could not make out what or who they were, but he guessed they were Indian, and in this country, should be Shoshone, unless it was another raid by one of the enemies of the people. But all the *Agaideka* had left together, and Shoots Running Buffalo and his men would already be far to the north. *Then who?* he asked himself, and he frowned, thinking of Little Mountain, *but he had a broken leg and wouldn't be riding so soon, even if he was vindictive, or would he?*

They were too far away to see any better, and it might be too dangerous to wait for them to come nearer. He knew he had to tell the others and prepare for the possibility that Little Mountain or someone else was on a vengeance quest and *they* might be the target. He slipped the scope in the case, slung the rifle at his back and started back to camp, wondering what should be done to prepare.

27 / VENGEANCE

"What color of horse did Little Mountain have?" asked Gabe, looking at Cougar Woman as she readied the cookfire for the first meal of the day.

She paused, frowning, "Why?"

"What color?" he asked again.

"He always rode a colorful black and white paint. He thought it made him look more powerful. But why do you ask?"

Gabe slowly nodded, looking at the others, "Because I saw some horses and men, below the ridge beyond the pass. They were too far to make out, but I saw a big paint horse and three or four others."

Ezra asked, "And you think it might be Little Mountain. But didn't he have a badly broken leg?"

Cougar Woman sat near Gabe, looking from him to Ezra and answered, "Yes. But he is one that has never been beaten and he would want vengeance. He would do what he must to get it. If there are others with him, it would be Snake Eater and any warrior that would believe his lies. Little Mountain would say anything to get others to follow and join him on a vengeance quest."

"It must be a terrible hate to make him come after us. It is not easy to ride with a bad leg, and the pain would be hard for anyone to take, unless it wasn't as bad as it looked." Gabe looked at Cougar, "Would he want to kill you?"

"Since he cannot have me, he would want to kill you and me," explained Cougar. "Snake Eater would not go against me, but he could not stand against Little Mountain."

Gabe stood, paced around the fire, thinking, then looked up at Ezra. "First off, we need to get Dove and Chipmunk in a safe place."

Dove frowned, "But I can fight!"

"Yes, but you can also get somewhere where you and the little pipsqueak will be safe. Maybe someplace where you can shoot from if necessary, but I'm sure Ezra agrees with me and wants you somewhere safe." Gabe glanced at Ezra, saw him nod his head in agreement, then stand and look around.

"What if both of us and our horses clear out, where it looks like just the two of you are here? Then we can find a spot where we can join the fight if necessary," suggested Ezra.

"Sounds good, but where do you think you could be?"

Everyone stood, looking around for possible positions that would provide cover and still give access to the camp and more. They discussed what places would be best and what action they should take, knowing that it would be best to end it all here, and not try to flee or avoid them. A man as vengeful as Little Mountain had proven himself to be, would be a man not easily discouraged in his pursuit of the source of his anger.

They quickly set about to prepare the camp and gear to appear as if only Gabe and Cougar Woman were at the camp and also positioned the needed weapons within easy access. It took but a few moments to set their plan in place, and Cougar Woman sat within reach of the pan and pot at the fire, while Gabe sat on a log near the big flat boulder they used the night before for the meat cutting. The smoke racks had been left in place, strips of meat still hung over the smoking coals, and Gabe sat with the rifle on his lap as if he were cleaning it. Tethered in the trees were Ebony, Gabe's big black and the blue roan pack horse, and the strawberry roan of Cougar's. But the horses were on long tethers and Ebony faced the fire, dropping his head to graze on the tall grass, when his head came up suddenly, ears forward, nostrils flaring, and eyes fixed on something in the black timber.

Gabe glanced at Cougar Woman, flicked his eyes toward the trees, and her slight nod acknowledged the action. Then a crashing of branches under hooves brought Gabe to his feet and Cougar to stand near the big rock, both looking toward the trees. The big paint horse pushed through the low hanging branches, Little Mountain sneering as he waved his lance and war shield. He stopped the horse, glared at Gabe, and faced Cougar Woman, "You will come with me, now!"

Cougar Woman stepped closer to Gabe, shielding the presence of her rifle that lay on the rock, and lifted her head to scowl at the intruder, "Hah! I will never go with you! You are a worm that should crawl in a hole and die! You are not a man!" she shouted the insults as her expression added vehemence to the invectives. She thrust one shoulder forward, "Who are you to make demands of me? I am his woman!" she nodded toward Gabe and made a slight step closer.

"Aiiieee!" screamed Little Mountain and dug heels to the paint horse causing him to lunge forward, crushing a smoke rack with his big hooves, and as Little Mountain jerked the horse's head to the side, the animal stumbled, but the strong arm of his rider pulled his head up and the horse kicked up the coals and ashes from the smoke fire, lifting a cloud of grey that startled the horse. But Little Mountain jerked him around again, lowered the tip of the lance and slapped his legs to the horse, wanting to drive at the hated white man and bury the lance in his side like a buffalo. But Gabe stepped to the side, not willing to shoot the horse and unable to see the big man lying low on the horse's neck, then rolled a stone underfoot and fell, but rolled away.

As the big renegade jerked the horse around for another try, Gabe had the sudden image of an ancient knight and his lance in a bout with another. Gabe grabbed for his pistol in his belt, but it was gone, lost as he rolled away from the charge. His rifle lay in the brush at the side, tossed there when he stumbled. Gabe grabbed at the tomahawk, still in his belt and stood, spread legged and crouched as Little Mountain charged.

Suddenly the bark of a rifle racketed through the camp and Little Mountain winced as the bullet from Cougar Woman's rifle plowed a furrow across his shoulder, drawing blood. The shot gave Gabe the chance to jump aside, and smash down on the lance as it passed, shattering the shaft and breaking the point. When Little Mountain reined the big paint to a stop at the trees, he cast aside the lance, grabbed his tomahawk from his belt and swung the big horse around for another charge.

Cougar Woman was frantically trying to reload her rifle. Gabe had dived toward the brush, grabbing for his rifle, and brought it up, only to see the frizzen open and no powder. He gave a quick look for the pistol but looked up to see Little Mountain bearing down on him again. Another rifle barked from the trees, but the brunt of the shot was taken by the war shield as it split with the impact, causing Little Mountain to shake it off his arm, blood showing on his shoulder where the bullet struck. But the renegade was driven by his lust for blood and vengeance, and dug heels into his horse, making it lunge forward as he lifted his tomahawk for a strike at Gabe's head.

But a streak of black came from the side and struck the big man, carrying him off the horse and into the dirt, and the teeth of Wolf were buried in the man's neck and the big black beast was bent on vengeance of his own as he ripped and tore the throat from the man beneath him. The growls and grunts from the two combatants filled the clearing and dust rose from the thrashing body of the man, moved by the muscular beast that grabbed for another mouthful of bloody meat on the face of the vengeful Shoshone.

Gabe called, "Wolf! Here!" and the big wolf snarled and growled as he stood astraddle of the body, then turned to look over his shoulder at his friend, then another glance at his quarry, and he slowly stepped back, still growling. He paused a moment, then turned and trotted to the side of Gabe, who dropped to his knees to throw his arms around the neck of his friend and run his fingers through the thick scruff. Cougar Woman came to the other side of the wolf and dropped beside him to give him a hug and show her love for the beast.

Ezra spoke, "Stay right there!" The tone of his command warned Gabe who reached for his rifle before he stood and turned to face the four warriors that had come from the trees, all afoot, but none with threatening weapons, although they all had bows and arrows held at their sides.

Snake Eater looked at the remains of Little Mountain, then at Cougar Woman. "We did not want this." The others did not speak or move, but their expressions were more of relief than hostility.

"Then why did you come with him?" asked Cougar Woman.

"He told us that this man had stolen you. He said your father did not want you to go with him, but he stole you. When Little Weasel and the council chose Lean Bear as war leader, he said he had to bring you back so they would know he should be war leader," explained Snake Eater.

"I did not think you would believe that, Snake Eater," suggested Cougar Woman. She looked from one to the other of the three who had come with Little Mountain, then turned back to Snake Eater, "Take that with you," pointing to the body of Little Mountain, "and tell Little Weasel what has happened. You can tell the council that I do not want them to send you away, but that is up to them, but you must go back, or you will be banished."

Snake Eater dropped his head, removed the arrow from the bow and replaced it in his quiver, prompting the others to do the same. Without any further conversation, they lifted the remains of the big man across his horse, tied his arms and feet together, and led the horse away. When they disappeared into the trees, everyone breathed a sigh of relief, and Ezra said, "I'm hungry!" The others laughed, shook their heads, and sat down near the fire pit, watching Dove as she rekindled the fire to warm up their food and coffee.

28 / CONSIDERATION

They made it a leisurely ride, wanting to remove themselves from the scene of the fight and go somewhere that was not haunted by images and memories. The magnificent scenery all about them took their thoughts elsewhere, although they traveled in silence. With the only sounds that of the plodding hooves, the occasional strike of a hoof on a stone, the intermittent blow from a horse, the creak of saddle leather, and the soft pads of Wolf as he kept pace with the horses. Until Cougar Woman, riding beside Gabe, looked at her man and asked, "Do you believe that the man that was killed," referring to Little Mountain and careful not to use the name of the dead as was the custom of her people, "will cross over to a better place?"

Gabe looked at her, sighed heavily and asked, "What do you believe?"

"Our people believe that a brave warrior will

cross over and fight for his people on the other side. That is why they are buried with their weapons and sometimes with their favorite horses." She paused a moment, "But, if the other side is the same, why should we have to cross over? I would hope that over there, it would be better than here."

Gabe thought a moment, rocking in his saddle with the gait of the big black stallion, and knew that Ezra and Dove were close behind him and could hear their conversation. He took some solace in that because he often deferred difficult questions to his friend, who had been raised in the church and whose father was a pastor.

They were winding through the thick black timber, tall spruce waving their tops in the slight breeze, fir and aspen standing firm, except the ever-quaking leaves of the white barked trees. A broad winged eagle soared overhead and as he banked on an updraft his chirping scream could be heard. With a quick glance at the majestic white-headed bird, Gabe looked back at Cougar and said, "We believe it is far better in Heaven. The bible tells us of its beauty, peace, joy, and the presence of loved ones and more. I do not believe there will be any fighting, although there will be tears, but those tears will be wiped away and any sadness will be replaced by joy."

"But, will someone like Little Mountain go to this place you call Heaven?" asked Cougar, frowning and concerned.

"There are two destinies, one is called Hell, the other Heaven. Those that are evil and have not chosen the right way and accepted Jesus as Savior, will go to Hell. In Hell there is no light, it is always burning but they will not be consumed, the only thing heard is screaming of pain and agony. But when anyone believes what the bible clearly teaches, and accepts the free gift of eternal life, they will spend eternity in Heaven."

Cougar thought about what her man had said, considering the different paths and where the dead reside, then frowned as she asked, "But you and I have killed many! My father said the black robes that came with the French said it was wrong to kill. Will we go to that place called Hell because we have done this?"

"Yes, the bible says '*Thou shalt not kill*' but that does not mean we are not to defend ourselves and our loved ones and friends. The bible is full of stories that happened long ago and tells of many battles and more where the good people killed others, but only to defend themselves or their family and friends."

She grew quiet as she considered, "When you killed the Blackfoot you were defending your people and me and my warriors." She paused and added, "And when we went after the Hidatsa, we were trying to get the captives back and had to kill to do that, and to defend ourselves." For a moment, she squinted her eyes as wrinkles marred her brow and then with eyes wide, she looked at Gabe, "So, we did not do a bad thing?"

"No, even though many died, we did not do a bad thing."

"So, we could still go to that Heaven?"

"Well, yes, but . . ."

"You said I must believe and accept . . . accept what?" she asked, frowning again.

"The free gift of eternal life offered by Jesus."

Cougar Woman reined up, leaned on the withers of her horse, "Where is this gift? I do not see a gift."

Gabe leaned back and withdrew the bible from his saddle bags, "It is told about in this book. When we stop and camp, I will show you, unless you want to take the time now."

She frowned at her man, she had seen him with this book before and knew he looked at it often, but she did not understand what it was and how he got anything from it. "Is the gift in there?" she asked, nodding toward the Bible.

"It tells about the gift in here, yes."

"Those are tracks you know? Like the tracks we see around us? I can see there," pointing to the tracks of Wolf in the dust beside the trail, "and know that a wolf passed here, and I know it is Wolf, because the pad on his front foot has a scar." She looked around, pointed to a yellow scar on a tall ponderosa bleeding sap, "That is the sign of a big grizzly bear. I know this because of the claw marks and how high it is, he marked his territory. I know that was done many sleeps ago because of the sap that drains." She looked at Gabe and at the bible, "Does that have tracks that you can tell about?"

Gabe smiled, nodding, "Yes, it has many tracks and I will show you what they mean."

"Good. Then we will know how to believe and accept as you say." She put leg pressure to her roan and started the group moving again.

Gabe knew she was curious, and they would again talk of this, and probably yet on this day when they camped. He smiled as he gigged Ebony to catch up to the roan as he leaned back to replace the bible in the saddle bags.

They had dropped from their camp by the ridge and ridden beside a long feeder creek that converged with the larger river below. They crossed on a gravel bar, the river only about thirty yards wide and no more than two feet deep, then took to a trail that followed the west bank. A long narrow mesa with scattered juniper and piñon stretched to a point where another stream converged from the west. When the big river bent to the northeast, they opted to go west, upstream of the fork that appeared to come from a low pass between two granite tipped sky scraping peaks. About a mile into the west valley, the stream forked, and they chose to follow the northernmost fork further up the valley. At the junction of two valleys, the stream forked again, with one coming from a higher valley and mountain range and the other carving its way down from the broad saddle that offered a pass to the western mountains.

They made camp above the fork and against the tree line of junipers. The tall grasses stretched to the stream bank and the trees at their back offered shelter, shade, and good cover. While the men stripped the animals of packs and saddles, the women set about making camp and gathering firewood. When the men finished rubbing down each of the horses and the mule, the women had coffee ready and Gabe and Ezra eagerly partook of the precious brew. Gabe took a long draught, frowned a mite, and looked at Ezra, "Have you been mixin' chicory with the coffee again?"

Ezra grinned, laughed, "Of course I have. Just how long did you expect that piddlin' amount of coffee you brought back would last?"

"You coulda warned me, instead o' just lettin' me swallow it down and pucker up!" grumbled Gabe. Although the chicory had its own distinctive taste that some preferred over coffee, the men preferred to mix the two and had become accustomed to the flavor, but Gabe's winter in St. Louis with straight coffee had dimmed his taste buds a mite and now it would take time to get back to enjoying the blend which had become the preferred taste of Ezra.

The women prepared an exceptional feast, fresh elk steaks broiled over the fire, baked yampa bulbs, and an assortment of ripe berries for their desert. When the meal was finished, Gabe and Ezra had their cups refilled and sat back when Dove sat beside her man and Cougar came beside Gabe, carrying his bible. She sat down, handed him the bible and said, "Show me."

"Show you? What in particular?"

"The tracks. The tracks that tell of this Heaven and the gift so I can believe and accept," explained Cougar, her stoic expression brokering no argument.

Gabe slowly nodded, took the bible and opened it to the fourteenth chapter of John and pointed at the printed words, "These are the tracks, and this is what they say, *"Let not your heart be troubled: ye believe in God, believe also in me. In my Father's house are many mansions: if it were not so, I would have told you. I go to prepare a place for you. And if I go and prepare a place for you, I will come again, and receive you unto myself; that where I am, there ye may be also. And whither I go ye know, and the way ye know."*

Cougar frowned, "What are 'mansions'?"

"Like a great big lodge, a building or house, a place to live when we're in Heaven with Him."

"It says you know the way, show me," she insisted.

Gabe smiled, twisted around a little to get more comfortable and turned to the book of Romans, chapter three. "There are four things you need to understand, the first is found here in verse twenty-three, *'For all have sinned, and come short of the glory of God.'* See Cougar, that just says all of us, you, me, Ezra, Dove, all of us have sinned and can't make it to Heaven on our own, that means we 'fall short' or don't quite make it, you know, like when you shoot an arrow at a target and it doesn't get there, it falls short."

"I understand, but what is 'sinned'?"

"That's when we've done wrong, done things we should not do, hurt others, things like that."

"And you have 'sinned'?" asked Cougar, frowning.

"We all have some time," confessed Gabe. "When we do wrong, or sin, that's what makes us 'fall short'."

Cougar slowly nodded her head, looked at the bible and motioned for him to continue. Gabe carefully took her through the steps that told about the penalty for sin, which is death, (Romans 6:23) and more than just dying and going to the grave, but eternity in Hell. She frowned at that but urged him to continue.

"Now, because the penalty for sin is death, that must be paid, so Jesus paid it for us so we wouldn't have to, see here in chapter five and verse eight, *'But God commendeth',* or showed, *'His love toward us, in that, while we were yet sinners, Christ died for us.'* See, He paid that price for us."

"Why? Why would he do that for me, He does not know me, and I do not know him?" asked Cougar very sincerely.

"That's just it, our God does know us and wants us to be with Him in Heaven. That's why he sent his son, Jesus, to pay the price for us so we could go to Heaven," explained Gabe.

Cougar frowned, looked from Dove to Ezra, then back to Gabe. She nodded for him to continue.

"Now, here in chapter six and verse 23, '... *but the gift of God is eternal life through Jesus Christ our Lord.'* That's the gift I told you about. And it is just like any gift, you have to accept it. See Cougar," he lifted his knife from the scabbard, "if I was to say this is a gift to you, and I kept it in my hand and you didn't take it, it wouldn't really be a gift. But, if you accept it and take it from my hand, then it would be yours. That's the same with this gift," he pointed at the words in the bible. "Here in chapter ten and verse nine, *'That if thou shalt confess with thy mouth the Lord Jesus, and shalt believe in thine heart that God hath raised him from the dead, thou shalt be saved.'* And down in verse thirteen, *'For whosoever shall call upon the name of the Lord shall be saved.'"*

Cougar had listened intently, watching Gabe as he read, her hand on his knee, and now she looked at him, "This 'confess' and 'call' does that mean to ask for the gift?"

"Yes."

"Will you show me how, tell me how?"

"Yes, I can do that now, if you want. But . . . I want you to be sure. See, here," he pointed to the verse again, "I want you to understand this where it says, 'believe in thine heart', Cougar, when I first saw you, I thought you were beautiful and I liked what I saw, but that was here," he tapped his forehead, "and later as I came to know you better, learn about you and your people and more, I liked what I learned. Again, that's here," tapping his head again. "And sometimes, people are like that with this," touching the scriptures, "they like it," tapping his head, "but it's not here," touching his chest near his heart. "When you and I learned more about one another, what I knew," tapping his forehead, "began to change to what I felt," touching his chest. "And as we were together more, that knowing became understanding and love. That's what the scriptures mean to 'believe in your heart' is to truly understand and believe with all that you are, just like I love you with all that I am and I believe you feel the same about me. I believe here," touching his chest again, "that I love you."

Cougar's frown lessened as her countenance changed to somber but still. She looked at Gabe, held her hand to her heart and said, "I do believe here," and paused, then continued, "but I must think here," tapping her forehead, "to be sure. This is not what my people have believed, and it is new to me. I like what I hear, and I believe it to be true, but I must think."

Gabe smiled, "It is good for you to think about it and if you have any questions, I will do my best to answer them and if I don't know," he nodded toward Ezra, "he will know."

29 / PLANS

Gabe walked to the top of the knoll to the north of their camp by the fading moonlight, Wolf at his side. The bald knob overlooked the little valley and their camp, unseen in the dim light, and he found himself a seat on a big rock that still held a little warmth from the previous day's hot sun. Wolf lay at his side as he turned to face the east, anticipating the first glimpse of the day's light and the Creator's morning painting. He sat the bible beside him, leaned his rifle against the stone, put his cased scope at his feet then leaned forward with elbows on his knees to begin his time in prayer.

As Gabe quietly voiced his petitions, Wolf stretched out, his face between his paws, and appeared to be praying as intently as his friend. Gabe glanced down at the black furball and smiled, then lifted his eyes to the thin grey line that marked the eastern horizon and the distant mountains that painted a jagged boundary in black. His thoughts returned to the many mornings he had spent with his Lord and friends, thinking of the times he and Pale Otter had spent together and her curiosity about the things of Scripture and the maker of all things. He mumbled a simple prayer that Cougar Woman would soon understand and decide in favor of the salvation offered by the Lord. Then as the sun began to paint the east, he reached for the bible, but paused when he saw Wolf's head come up and the black beast look to the back of the knoll, then drop his head unconcerned.

Gabe smiled, guessed it to be Cougar Woman coming and he lay the bible in his lap and turned the pages to the book of John, chapter three. Cougar Woman stepped up behind him, "I know you know I am here."

"Ummhmmm," he said, as he scooted to the side, offering her a seat beside him. He looked up at her as she stood at the edge of the rock, then turned to sit beside him. She looked at the colors of the sky, turned to Gabe, "I want to do that."

"Do what?"

"Accept that gift so I will know that I will go to Heaven when I die," she answered.

Gabe smiled, reached his arm around her, smelling the freshness of the woman, the odor of soap about her and the light fragrance of columbines. She often used the bloom of flowers to freshen her hair after her usual morning bathing and washing her hair. He breathed deep of her and said, "Alright. Here's what we'll do. I'll pray aloud, and you can pray with me, but only as you really want to and believe, understand?"

"Yes," she answered, simply, nodding.

Gabe lowered his head and closed his eyes, keeping his arm around her and clasping her hand in his, and began to pray. "Father in Heaven, we come to you with willing and believing hearts . . ." and continued to give thanks to the Lord, then spoke to Cougar, "Now, if you believe with all your heart, just repeat these words, but only if you believe," he paused just a moment, then continued, "I want to trust you today," then paused for her to say in her own way, much the same, and continued through the prayer to ask forgiveness for sins and to accept the free gift of eternal life that would give her Heaven when she died. Cougar Woman said the prayer in her own unique wording, and when they finished, both said "Amen."

Gabe looked at his woman and tears had made a trail down her cheeks, but she smiled up at him and said, "Thank you, thank you. I know what we did was right, I feel it right here," she tapped her heart. "Is that the way you felt when you did it?"

Gabe pulled her close, "Yes, it is. But it's not the feeling, it's the knowing as well. Now let me show you a very special verse." He pulled the bible close and began to read, "'*For God so loved the world that he gave his only begotten Son, that whosoever believeth in him should not perish, but have everlasting life.'* See, He gave his son, to pay the price for our sin, and now, because of what you've just done, you have everlasting, or eternal life, to live forever in Heaven with Him."

"I do not understand everything, but I do know what you have shown and told me, and I do believe." She looked up at Gabe, smiling, "Thank you." She looked down at the bible, "Now, you must teach me what these tracks mean."

Gabe nodded, "I will. But, it will take some time, but I know you will learn and probably more quickly that I suspect." He glanced at the sunrise, thought about the new day and the beginning of a new life for Cougar Woman and a new life for the both of them together, and let a slow smile paint his face as he considered what the future might hold for them. He stood, offered her his hand and she stood beside him, wiping the tears from her face, lay her head on his chest, then they followed Wolf back to camp.

A cool breeze came from the mountains as they dropped from the knoll, making both Gabe and Cougar Woman shiver just a bit, and they eagerly went to sit beside the fire. As soon as they were seated, they held their hands to the fire and Cougar Woman looked at Dove, smiling, and said, "I prayed to God above and asked for the gift! Now I know I will go to Heaven, like you!"

Dove came quickly to her side and the two women embraced, and Dove said, "That makes me happy. I am glad for you."

"Me too!" declared Ezra, walking back into camp just in time to hear the news. He sat beside Gabe as Cougar Woman joined Dove in the preparation of their breakfast. Dove already had some cornpone baking in the dutch oven and Cougar Woman hung some strips of elk meat from the willow sticks beside the fire. Gabe and Ezra had their ever-present cups of coffee in their hands as they watched the concert of harmony as the women worked in unison.

Ezra looked at Gabe, "So, we still headin' north?"

"Sounds good to me, you?"

"Ummhmm, but did you feel that cool breeze off the mountain this mornin'?"

"I did, but we are pretty high up, you know," observed Gabe.

"I'm thinkin' it's a warning that there's a cold winter comin', and we ain't got no place to lay our heads! If you recall, we left the only lodge we had back in the trees of the encampment."

"Remember what Shoots Running Buffalo told us about the different territories?"

"Yeah, what about 'em?"

"The way I figger, we're kinda walking the line between the Blackfoot, the Salish, the Pend d'Oreille, and the Nez Perce. But of that bunch, I think the Pend d'Oreille and Nez Perce are the most peaceable." He paused, twisted on his seat and looked to the west, "If we keep on west, we'll cross the middle fork and west fork of the three forks. Then somewhere further should be the headwaters of the Big Hole or the Salmon. That would put us in either *Agaideka* Shoshone country or Nez Perce. Then we could start lookin' for someplace to spend the winter." Gabe paused as he lifted his eyes to the morning sky, he knew they were usually on the trail by now, but there was no hurry, at least not yet.

Ezra answered, "You thinkin' a cavern or buildin' a cabin, or what?"

"Yeah."

Ezra twisted on his seat, glared at Gabe, "Yeah, what?!" he spouted.

Gabe chuckled at his friend, "A cavern or a cabin or something like we did back on the Popo Agie. That was a comfortable winter we spent there, wasn't it?"

Ezra shook his head, "Yeah, it was. But it was also a lot of work. And although a cabin can be mighty comfortable, a cavern takes less work."

Gabe lifted his eyes to the sky again, "And I'm thinkin' you're right about it bein' a cold and hard winter. So, we're further north, and these are some mighty tall mountains, so I reckon it will be one of those almighty cold wilderness winters."

Ezra dropped his eyes to the fire, thinking about all that would be necessary. The building of a cabin, or fixing up a cavern, laying in winter meat, which would mean getting a fat bear for both his pelt and his fat as

well as venison and more, and they were already past
the middle of summer. He looked up at Gabe, "So, we
start lookin' for a place soon?"

"I'd say right away, but preferably out of Blackfoot
country!"

"Then I guess we better start by fattenin' up our
own selves!" declared Ezra, licking his lips at the
sight of Dove removing the lid from the dutch oven
to reveal the golden-brown cornbread.

***

They made good time for a short day with a late start.
After crossing the saddle above their camp, Gabe
looked at Ezra, pointing to the long valley below
them, "Looks like that valley will take us to the middle
fork. Should make it 'fore nightfall."

Ezra looked where Gabe pointed, noted the timbered
foothills on either side of the steep sided valley. On the
north and south of their chosen route, tall mountains
poked their hoary heads above timberline, some still
holding small patches of white, glaciers that wouldn't
disappear until late summer, if ever. He looked back at
Gabe, "Yeah, we should be able to do that, long as we
don't run into any unexpected visitors."

Cougar Woman looked back at Ezra, "Like Blackfoot?"
Dove added, "Or grizzlies?"

"Yeah, somethin' like that," he agreed.

But the rest of the day offered nothing but the raw beauty of unexplored wilderness. The trail followed the muddy creek, made so by the recent warmth that melted a bit more of the snowpack, and worked its way through the black timber. They broke from the pines just past mid-day and chose to cross the wide valley. They left the greenery of the valley of the middle fork behind and started into the desolate sand and adobe hills and by dusk had found a good camp beside a creek and with timber on the south slope of the narrow valley. Gabe thought that it was one thing to travel in the mountains, or even in the green river bottomed valleys, but the dusty rolling hills that held little more than cacti and sage, were difficult on the horses and the riders. He slapped at his buckskins, causing a cloud of dust to lift and he fanned it away, then looked at Cougar, "I bet you're anxious to get into that creek, am I right?" he asked as he nodded toward the willow lined creek on the far side of the valley bottom.

Cougar Woman said, "I would like to get clean before we cook."

"That's fine with me, and I'm sure the horses won't mind either!" He slapped the neck of the big black that now looked almost like Dove's buckskin. Dust lifted and he shook his head and led the way to the creek. They let the horses drink first, then stepped down and stripped the gear from the animals and led them into the water, splashing water on them to rid them of the dust and grime of the trail and all the horses dipped their noses deep and splashed around on their own. When they finished with the animals, they tethered each one to the willows then started upstream with some yucca root soap and blankets to use as towels and with the men downstream of the women, they all enjoyed a refreshing bath.

They took the time to wash their clothes while they bathed, then donned their fresh sets and soon emerged from their respective backwater pools, everyone smiling at the relief. It was a quick meal of the left-overs from breakfast, but it was satisfying and after a short spell by the fire, they turned in for the night, vigilant horses and Wolf nearby.

30 / SEARCH

With an early start, they pushed out of the rolling foothills and into the grassy bottom of a wide valley that ran north and south, but Gabe's early morning reconnoiter prompted them to stay near the small rambling river in the valley bottom and avoid the dry skirted shoulders of the taller mountains to the west. With two more days on the trail they crossed the west fork of the rivers, then crested a low saddle where before them opened up a wide fertile valley, framed by a long range of tall mountains on the west and a horseshoe basin on the south.

Gabe reined up and waited for the others to join him on the crest as he leaned forward on the pommel of his saddle, forearms crossed as he took in the panorama. "I think this will be a good place," he said, then looked at the others who were also taking in the vista. Gabe pointed to an island like formation of two parallel hills, timbered on the north slopes and flanked by a feeder creek that ran north into the larger stream in the valley bottom. "But for right now, I think that rise yonder," pointing to the hills below, "would make a good starting point for a camp, at least for a day or so, till we scout around a bit more."

Ezra stood in his stirrups, shading his eyes, "Lookee yonder, by the river," pointing to the north of the hills below, "ain't that a herd of elk?"

Cougar Woman had shaded her eyes and looked, answering, "Yes, and there are antelope nearer the river."

Gabe looked at the others, "So, what do you think, are we in Shoshone or Pend d'Oreille country?"

Cougar Woman said, "I think Shoots Running Buffalo was wrong when he said the Pend d'Oreille were there," nodding her head toward the upper end of the long valley, "my father said the Sélis, who are close to the Pend d'Oreille, live in this country, and the Pend d'Oreille are further north. They are like the Bannock and the Shoshone; they are allies and often intermarry."

Gabe turned to look at his woman, "Are the Sélis friendly?"

Cougar shrugged, and Gabe knew he had asked an unanswerable question. Any people can be friendly or prone to war, depending on the leaders of the bands and the circumstances of the times. He and Ezra had experienced both the unity and conflict between neighboring tribes many times.

"Well, if we're gonna winter here, let's hope their leaders are the friendly kind," resolved Gabe, gigging Ebony off the slope and starting toward the chosen campsite.

***

Although they camped on the east flank of the timbered hills, early the next morning they climbed to the crest together, all anxious for a good look around at their home territory. They sat together, the women with legs drawn up and arms around their knees, Gabe and Ezra seated and leaning back on outstretched arms. They had a time of prayer together before the sun showed its first light, but now they sat quietly together, basking in the beauty of the Creator as He painted the eastern sky with muted pinks and oranges, sending several lances of gold high above.

"If we split up and scout these draws and such, we could find us a good spot pretty soon, don'tcha think?" suggested Ezra.

"Ummhmm, and we need to look for good timber, lodgepole pine would be best, year-round water, pasture for the horses, and such," he paused, looking at Ezra and his smirk as he listened, "I know, you already know what we need, I was just thinkin' out loud."

"I'd still rather find a good cave, mebbe save us some back breakin' work," added Ezra.

Gabe chuckled at his friend, then stood to look around. He pointed to the south, "Me'n Cougar will scout those two valleys yonder," then looking north of the valleys indicated, "And if you'n Dove scout those valleys coming from the peaks there," pointing west toward the long line of granite tipped peaks, "then we can be back in camp 'fore dark and see if'n we need to scout more or . . ." he shrugged as he made one more scan of the big valley.

***

As dusk was settling in, Gabe and Cougar returned to camp to find Ezra and Dove waiting near the fire. Dove had put together a stew in the pot hanging over the flames and stood stirring as Ezra leaned back against the rock with a cup of coffee steaming near his chin. "So, what'd ya find?"

Gabe stepped down, took the reins of Cougar's roan as she slid to the ground, and started to the trees to strip the gear from the two horses. Ezra followed and Gabe answered, "Some mighty pretty country, but nothing that suited me for a cabin or such." He loosened the girth on his saddle, pulled it off the big black as Ezra stood holding his coffee and grinning. Gabe saw his smirk and said, "Alright, what'd you find?"

"I think I found us a good spot. There is a cave, but it's not big enough for all that we need, but it would be a good place to hang meat and store gear. Lotsa trees, spruce, fir and lodgepole. A nice spring fed lake, looks deep enough so it wouldn't freeze solid. Pasture above and below the lake and several meadows for the horses. Dove liked it!"

Come morning, Ezra was so sure that Gabe and Cougar Woman would like their choice of cabin sites, he suggested they take the pack horses and all the gear with them. Gabe looked at his friend, shrugged his shoulders and said, "No harm in that. If it's all you say it is, we can get started, and if not, we can always camp there and keep lookin'."

Ezra frowned, "Well, ain't chu just a bundle of positivity this mornin'?"

The men were sitting near the cookfire, having finished their breakfast and enjoying their coffee, and Gabe grabbed a small stick and threw it at his friend, making him jerk to the side and spill his coffee. Both men laughed and went to get the horses and mule rigged and loaded so they could start their day's sojourn.

It was mid-morning when they entered the mouth of the valley. Gabe stopped, looking up the long valley that lay between two forested ridges. The valley lay north and south, with the south end rising to the tall mountains, the north end or mouth of the valley opening to the wide river bottomed valley where they now sat. The long ridge on the left was slightly higher than the one on the right or west that also had a steep talus slope devoid of timber that marked the crest and rode the ridge for about a mile or two. From where they were, they could not see the lake Ezra mentioned, and he explained, "It's about two, three miles further on. The place where I think the cabin should be, is on the shoulder of that west ridge overlooking the lake and valley."

"Does it back up to the cave you mentioned?" asked Gabe.

"Ummhmm, we could even use the face of the ridge where the cave is as the back wall of the cabin."

They rode into the long valley, taking in everything they saw. The women pointed out the berry bushes, patches of flowers and the many edibles, and likely places for rabbits. Gabe was looking at the tall grasses for the horses, the sign of passing elk, deer and more, pleased with everything he saw. As Ezra led the way into the trees above the lake, Gabe noted the lodgepole pine, the tall thin and straight growing pines that were excellent for roof timbers and even the small ones for chinking. A thicket of mature lodgepole offered logs for the cabin, and the many spruce, tall and straight, would be used for the walls and ridgepoles. As they neared the edge of the talus slope, Gabe noted the flat lichen covered stone that would be good for the fireplace, and Ezra pointed out the thicket of scrub oak that shielded the entrance to the cave.

When they stepped down and started looking the site over, the level of excitement seemed to rise

as each one pointed out trees, rocks, views, everything they had wanted for a cabin site and then they
stood together, and agreed, "Yup, this is the place,"
acknowledged Gabe, as the others nodded and smiled,
and they laughed together, a laughter of relief and
hope and excitement about the coming days as they
would build their home together in this land so full
of promise.

***

For three and a half weeks, they worked from can
see to can't see, everyone doing their part and more.
Felling trees, peeling logs, cutting notches, raising
walls one log at a time, laying lodgepoles for the roof,
overlaying that with sod, splitting logs to make shut-
ters and doors, gathering mossy mud for chinking
and covering that with small poles, but as they laid
on the last bit of sod for the roof, they stepped back
and admired their work. It was a beautiful sight to the
hard-working couples, nestled against the talus slope,
the back door opening into their cold storage cave.
They had found another way out of the cave that was
higher up the slope and well concealed, offering both
an outlet for any smoke in the cave and a possible escape route if needed. The clearing that held the cabin
was made so by the cutting of the timber to build
the structure that was hidden from view from below

but the thin trees at the east and downhill side, gave them a view of the valley that would tell of anyone's approach. The cabin had three rooms, a bedroom for each couple and a common room that held the fireplace and counter for the cookware and more.

Gabe and Ezra looked at their handiwork with pride, knowing they didn't do it by themselves for the women worked hand in hand with the men every day. But now, they would fashion the necessary beds and table, saving any other work for idle winter hours. And as Gabe stood, his arm around Cougar Woman's waist, she said, "Now we must hunt. The time of snow will soon come, and we must have much meat and more."

Gabe looked down at her, although she was only about four inches shorter, and said, "Ummhmm, and after all this," nodding to the cabin, "hunting will be plumb pleasant!"

Ezra asked, "So, what do you figger, end of August, first of September?"

Gabe shrugged, "Yeah, 'bout that. I noticed some aspen startin' to turn colors, and some buck brush showin' red, so, September, I reckon."

"Ummhmm, and I heard some bulls buglin' this morning. So, that means we gotta do some serious huntin' then."

"Yeah, but we also need to be vigilant about any hunting parties, at least until we know if they're gonna be friendly or not," cautioned Gabe. "That's all we need is to get some band upset and go on the warpath in the middle of winter!"

"Nope, wouldn't like that at all!" agreed Ezra.

***

It was a time of promise and hope for them all. The promise of good times to come and a warm home for the winter season, and hope for many more times together, exploring and discovering. It was a good time to be together in a beautiful land that gave so much hope.

A LOOK AT: WINTER WARPATH (STONECROFT SAGA BOOK 9)

It was supposed to be a cozy winter in their new cabin, but it started with a cantankerous silvertip grizzly wreaking havoc on everything. That would prove to be the least of their problems in the coming winter…

After a trading foray to visit their neighbors, the Salish, two days north, everything seemed to get turned upside down. They found themselves in contested territory with a band of honor seeking young bucks from the Siksika band that sought to gain scalps and captives from their sworn enemies, the Salish. And that wasn't enough to upset their peaceful plans, but when Gabe, or Spirit Bear, found out the Blackfoot had stolen the mares bred by his stallion and were carrying foals that belonged to him, it became personal.

AVAILABLE SEPTEMBER 2020

ABOUT THE AUTHOR

Born and raised in Colorado into a family of ranchers and cowboys, B.N. Rundell is the youngest of seven sons. Juggling bull riding, skiing, and high school, graduation was a launching pad for a hitch in the Army Paratroopers. After the army, he finished his college education in Springfield, MO, and together with his wife and growing family, entered the ministry as a Baptist preacher.

Together, B.N. and Dawn raised four girls that are now married and have made them proud grandparents. With many years as a successful pastor and educator, he retired from the ministry and followed in the footsteps of his entrepreneurial father and started a successful insurance agency, which is now in the hands of his trusted nephew. He has also been a successful audiobook narrator and has recorded many books for several award-winning authors. Now finally realizing his life-long dream, B.N. has turned his efforts to writing a variety of books, from children's picture books and young adult adventure books, to the historical fiction and western genres.